PRAISE FOR PETER KISPERT'S

I KNOW YOU KNOW WHO I AM

"Engrossing, unsettling, full of characters in search of their place in the world, *I Know You Know Who I Am* reminds me in the best possible way of the debut collections of Mary Gaitskill and Adam Haslett, in tone and talent and the promise of what will come next."

—David Ebershoff, *New York Times* bestselling author of *The Danish Girl* and *The 19th Wife*

"This debut collection has a wisdom and a tapestry of language far beyond the author's years. Loosely linked unreliable narrators remind us that we might find religion in the most unlikely places—such as the space between a truth and a lie."

—Jodi Picoult, *New York Times* bestselling author of *A Spark of Light* and *Small Great Things*

"Peter Kispert's dazzling collection is a reminder that fiction tells lies in order to discover truth."

—Garrard Conley, *New York Times* bestselling author of *Boy Erased*

"If I could give the characters in Peter Kispert's expansive, funny, and moving collection the forgiveness and recognition they seek, I would do so wholeheartedly. These unforgettable stories look head on at the spectacles we make of our lives and the impossibility of turning away from them. A talent to watch."

—Danielle Lazarin, author of *Back Talk*

"Sometimes you read a collection and you wonder how a mere mortal wrote it because the language is so pure, the depth of emotion so profound—Peter Kispert is a wizard, creating a collection of liars and lies that will ring true in the heart of any reader. A tour de force: read this book."

—Nick White, author of *How to Survive a Summer* and *Sweet & Low*

"Lashed by years and bound by love, the liars in this incredible debut punish themselves as their compulsions and betrayals tremble across time. Cut crosswise, their lives show these pathologies at work, just as hard and irradiating, superheated and sad, as the prose in which they're rendered. Above all, it is through Kispert's immense talent that we come to understand, and even love, who they are." —Patrick Nathan, author of *Some Hell*

PENGUIN BOOKS

I KNOW YOU KNOW WHO I AM

PETER KISPERT's fiction and nonfiction has appeared in *OUT* magazine, *GQ*, *Esquire*, *Playboy*, *The Carolina Quarterly*, *The Journal*, *Slice*, and elsewhere. He is a graduate of Indiana University's MFA program, where he taught undergraduate fiction writing workshops, and an assistant editor at *American Short Fiction*. He lives in New York.

peterkispert.com

I KNOW YOU KNOW WHO I AM

WHO I AM

Stories

PETER KISPERT

 PENGUIN BOOKS

PENGUIN BOOKS
An imprint of Penguin Random House LLC
penguinrandomhouse.com

The following stories were published previously in different forms: "I Know You
Know Who I Am" in *The Journal*; "Puncture" in *Ninth Letter*; "Aim for the
Heart" in *Slice Magazine*; "Audition" (as "Audition #21") in *Devil's Lake*;
"Please Hold" in *Joyland*; "Be Alive" in *Passages North*;
"Breathing Underwater" in *The Carolina Quarterly*; "Diving, Drifting" in
South Dakota Review; and "Double Edge" (as "The Vanishing") in *Tin House*.

LIBRARY OF CONGRESS CATALOGING-IN-PUBLICATION DATA
Names: Kispert, Peter, author.
Title: I know you know who I am : stories / Peter Kispert.
Description: New York : Penguin Books, An imprint of Penguin Random House
LLC, 2019. | Identifiers: LCCN 2019016016 (print) | LCCN 2019019392 (ebook) |
ISBN 9780525506058 (ebook) | ISBN 9780143134282 (paperback)
Subjects: LCSH: Gay men—Identity—Fiction. | Deception—Fiction. |
Intimacy (Psychology)—Fiction. | Psychological fiction.
Classification: LCC PS3611.I8726 (ebook) | LCC PS3611.I8726 A6 2019 (print) |
DDC 813/.6—dc23
LC record available at https://lccn.loc.gov/2019016016

Printed in the United States of America
1   3   5   7   9   10   8   6   4   2

Set in Stempel Garamond LT Pro
Designed by Gretchen Achilles

For Brick Kyle

CONTENTS

Mistrust is the fuel for so much mental pain, so many mental disorders. I am not talking here about the suspicions we sometimes have of one another, the distant but lurking sense that perhaps our lover lies to us, our best friend whispers behind our back. I am talking about a belief that betrayal inundates the atoms of the universe, is so woven into the workings of the world that every step is treacherous, and that below the rich mud lies a mine.

—LAUREN SLATER,
Welcome to My Country

Part I

I KNOW

I KNOW YOU KNOW
WHO I AM

It's a true story because it's a story I tell myself. But you want the story with the true facts, the stuff I can prove, and even though that's impossible—well, here it is.

When I asked a stranger to pretend to be Finn, just for ten minutes, I was surprised he agreed to. Turns out he was an actor with some small theater—always up for a challenging role.

My boyfriend Luke had been in the bathroom fixing his hair while I appraised potential Finns in the coffee shop—the kind of man, I imagined, whose careful attention to his sideburns suggested his biting sarcasm. Having spent the last three weeks trying to cast him over the Internet, the Finn I'd hired was a no-show, which left me minutes to find and coach. I was searching for a particular face, one that simultaneously read *I've seen some shit* and *I'm pretty hilarious*. I was also looking at a lot of eyebrows; the more expressive, the better—it was the one physical detail about Finn I'd accidentally let slip.

"Here," I said, sliding a black-and-white photo of a model toward the man: dark, swooping hair, a smile that seemed impossibly sincere (though now he seemed to be laughing at me), a chiseled chest. I'd clipped the photo from one of the magazines Luke shoots for, or used to shoot for, before the incident that got him fired. "Go off this."

"Is this him?" he asked.

"That's you."

He smiled. The man clearly hadn't seen success as an actor. A teenage girl looked on, witnessing the bizarre transaction. I rolled my eyes at her, letting her know I saw.

The story behind Finn had been stitched irregularly and out of necessity into a complex fabric of a lie, a thing so false it now seemed absolutely true. Where I was in the story of Finn depended on who I was with. He became an excuse to miss work, to cancel plans last minute—fleeting moments that held small thrills at their candy centers. The story of Finn with Luke had been mostly written; just never entirely finished. I planned to cut ties with him in a few weeks, or to maybe kill him off somehow, in a car crash or by way of some little-known cancer, an accidental overdose, something like what happened to my father. This was all to say: I had lied. I had made him up.

"Okay," I said, trying to relax. "In a few minutes, my boyfriend will be out of the bathroom, and he's going to ask you questions. He just wants to make sure you're real."

I briefly summarized Finn's situation as Luke knew it: He is living with two friends here in New York; he misses me; he is sick but pretending to be on the mend; he listens to indie rock and doesn't need to honor questions about our relationship, citing instead that he is *still processing* a recent fight over why he isn't considering chemo. He once fell off a canoe with me at midnight while wearing only a plastic gold smock. But that's not important.

"Ian!" Luke's voice carried over the hiss of the espresso machine.

"Found him! Hiding behind a newspaper," I called back, giving the man a *You're on* look. I tapped the back of the chair, thinking of that beautiful smile, trying to replicate it as I slid the photo back into my pocket. I looked to Luke, who walked toward me, drying his hands on his jeans. My breath hitched in my chest.

"Typical Finn," I said, and watched as they shook hands.

Finn was born on one of our first dates—or, the idea of him was. We were eating at a new chain family restaurant, its walls covered in faux-dated decor, worn horseshoes and skis. Luke asked if I had friends in Burlington, and I said I did. Truthfully, I didn't. I'd resigned myself to being alone, managing a bakery, living a largely abstinent gay lifestyle, and watching bad reality television religiously every night. My loneliness embarrassed me deeply, constant proof of my unlovability. Luke asked what my friends' names were, and suddenly imagined people came bursting forth: Jessica, Lindsay, Andrew (who goes by Andy), Finn.

"Finn," he said, flicking condensation off his glass. "I like that name."

"Yeah," I said. "He's a pretty cool guy."

As it turns out, *Pretty cool guy* is dangerous territory. *Pretty cool guy* is lighting the fuse.

It wasn't that I'd never lied before, or even that my lies weren't frequent. They were. The problem was that I'd made this person, this ghost, who could walk through the walls of my life, disorienting and rearranging, forcing me to recalculate every time Luke asked about him, which was often. And even more of a problem—it was *working*: Luke believed me. If I wanted him to think I was generous, I could work into conversation that Finn had been in some trouble with his landlord and I'd bailed him out. If I wanted him to think I had self-control, I'd explain that there had been another incident and Finn needed to learn I couldn't do everything for him. After a few months, I had given Finn his own, terrifying breath. Luke said he wanted to meet him, maybe take some headshots for casting calls. (At that point, Finn was trying his hand at acting.)

Pretty cool guy.

"He's kind of a loner," I'd said. I was very aware it wasn't true, that even this particular ghost of a human would be loud and inviting, unrestrained.

"Well, when he's back in the area," he'd said. And I'd nodded like I meant it.

The moment ended and I watched him eat, the careless way he considered his plate comforting me into the knowledge he had believed me once more. Luke finished his meal, and I pushed my potatoes around enough to look like they'd been at least seriously considered.

"Wonder whose family this is," he said, pointing to a

photo fixed to the wall behind a stand of menus. I knew instantly it was posed: a bunch of restaurant employees fitted in old uniforms, filtered through grayscale. The kids didn't look like the parents at all. The photo's edge had a hard diagonal crease. I could see someone making it, easy.

"Probably no one's," I said. "Probably fake."

On our way out the door, I noticed that same photo above the doorframe—the same crease, the same family. On the drive back to my apartment, I said, "You know, I think that *was* a real family photo." I had no idea of what prompted me to say this, but something in me wanted to inch closer to showing that I had the truth; only I knew those people could not have been related, and that I could prove it.

"Yeah, I think so too," he said, nodding. The light turned green, and the truth stayed behind us.

We were hiking in the Adirondacks when Luke caught the first lie.

Overhead, sunlight shone through the leaves in mottled greens, and wind rushed through the trail. It had been nearly a year since we had begun dating, and I was falling for him—had been since I first saw him, really. Luke was talking about how he'd get the perfect shot at the marble crown of the mountaintop, how he wanted us to take a photo together, something to remember the day by and to prove to his friends on the coast we were dating. I found it funny those friends didn't, couldn't, believe him when he'd told them about me, weeks before—a kind of endearing vulnerability, though I wasn't sure if he saw his admission that way. I guessed, swatting a fly away from my ear, that he was just telling me the truth.

"That'll be nice," I said. "We do need a photo. This is my first real hike, you know."

He gave me a look, figuring something out, and paused. I wasn't able to tell if he was catching his breath or catching me, in the middle of my story.

"I thought you said you went camping with Finn. That time in New Hampshire."

A flock of geese passed in formation overhead, their caws echoing. He furrowed his brow.

"Oh, that," I said, summoning a laugh to suggest some funny memory, some distant thing I'd only now brought into focus. "Yeah, but I mean really hiking."

Luke squinted, suspicious for a moment.

"Okay," he said, and lifted the lens to his eye. "Turn to your left. Two steps back. Watch your arms. Good, just like that. And smile."

"So, how long have you been in New York City?"

Luke had a list of questions, and with the delivery of each came a quiet shudder. If the lie collapsed, if Finn was revealed to be the empty shell he was, Luke would stop seeing me. It was only after he figured out I wasn't allergic to dairy like I'd claimed that he demanded he meet Finn. His suspicions about god knows what else I'd told him had led him to ask me to get ice cream with him one night, at a place next to a mini golf course. Beetles and moths dumbly buzzed and struck the tall lamp next to the counter, which cast a harsh orange glow onto us as we waited for our cones. I could tell something in him had shifted then, saddened, and he explained what I had mentioned, months ago, about the time my neck swelled up from only a sip of milk. On the way home, the air in the car constricted me. As we pulled up the driveway, he said that he needed to know I was not capable of such flagrant deceit.

So there I was: willing a lie into being.

"Oh, four months or so," the man said. It was—astonishingly, thankfully—an acceptable response. He did some weird stage flourish with his hair. It looked like acting.

"Are you living around here?"

"Yeah, with a few friends."

"And how's the acting going?"

"Well, it's—it's going."

There was a moment of real sadness in his face, when this stranger was quietly revealed. Through the heart of the moment, all I thought was: Thank God, something genuine.

A family moved to the small table next to us, crowding with extra chairs.

And that's when I saw her.

Of all the coffee shops in New York, of all the people, my high school prom date, Diane, was sitting among them—her blond hair like a bird's nest, her sputtering laughter, her fit frame all still intact, though weathered, aged. My stomach tightened, as if I'd ingested bad milk. If I really had met Finn as a sophomore like I'd said, Diane would've known him, even just his name, his vague presence. I considered how I might obviate the problem—maybe Finn had changed his name? Who did this man look like, and why could I not summon him among my old classmates? I felt pale, vulnerable, caught in the crevasse between truth and fiction.

Turning back, I saw Luke nodding at something Finn said, strangely at ease, and I began to wonder whether he'd figured out the whole thing was a ruse. When given the upper hand in the past, though, Luke had always made a point to show it—mentioning how bad my chess move was or how I could've saved more money at a restaurant. I moved my chair carefully away from Diane, which placed me directly opposite Luke.

"So," Luke said, ripping a straw wrapper. "Tell me about Ian."

And then: me. Of course.

Luke had lost his job in a fit of rage for being "too honest" with a model about her poses, which he considered stiff and ugly. This from the same man who slept with me, a "stocky" (his generous word for it) five-foot-six ex-wrestler who tried and gave up yoga on several different occasions for being unable to hold even basic poses.

"You'd think they'd want a good shot," he said, reaching for a wineglass. "You think they'd, like, just want me to be honest."

"I thought you threw something."

"It was a lens. It was just a lens."

He poured himself a glass of wine; he had a habit of reaching blindly for a bottle in the cheap section of the grocery store and finding whatever he'd purchased disappointing.

"Good wine," he said, acknowledging the glass. "Want some?"

"No, thanks," I said. "I'm not into red." But actually, I didn't mind it. I had chained myself to this new detail I had to follow to its dead end, no matter the cost. The me here, and the me out in the riptide. I had taken to lying not just about Finn, but the minutiae of my life, things that would never return to either of us, that would just drift away unseen, unnoted.

Which was, I knew even then, a warning sign.

"Well, Ian here wants me to go to chemo," Finn said, smiling. He clapped my thigh and forced a short, loud laugh. The man was probably the worst actor in a ten-mile radius. Which was, in New York, saying something.

"So he's told me," Luke said. "Sorry to hear, by the way." He pushed away the torn scraps of straw wrapper.

"Oh, it's fine," the man said.

I wanted to take this man aside, to lecture him on proper use of the word "fine," and how—the way I'd described it—he was not, in fact, fine. He was four or five years, tops. Maybe next week if I could kill him off and save Luke from ever uncovering the truth: that there is no Finn. Just this "actor," "acting."

As if by some unreal cue, a stage direction written right into the story itself, I heard Diane spill her coffee. The sudden screech of moving chairs as she reached for napkins.

The perfect time, I thought, to clean a filthy floor. To look up and notice me.

Luke met me after he'd had—in his words—*the best crois- sant since he lived in Paris*, back when he thought he could make it big, debuting in one of those foreign glossies. He bought the pastry earlier in the day, before work, and I'd remembered his token indecision, his tan skin, serious ha- zel eyes, camera case in hand. I'd tried to flirt with him by asking if he wanted samples of a new truffle, but he didn't hear me. Which was probably for the best. (As it turned out, they dried out your mouth; a few customers in this way choked, quietly gagging, out of the store.)

He came back in while I was closing, turning up chairs onto the tables and sweeping. I usually brushed the dirt to the corners and blamed the cashier for it, but when I saw him again, I grabbed the dustbin.

"Are you closed?" he asked, having ignored the un- missable sign I'd turned on the door that read in blocky red letters: CLOSED. "Sorry to intrude."

"Closing," I said. "And it's fine."

"Just wanted to ask—are your croissants made from scratch?"

"Yeah, every morning."

"You make them?"

I stopped for a moment, leaning down to collect a small pyramid of dirt. I was trying not to give in to my impulse to tell him yes, it was me, but I felt it tickle out of me, a reflex I couldn't control. "Yeah."

A lie, of course. He introduced himself, and we got to talking about how croissants are properly made. I invented something idiotic about the importance of using fresh eggs. His smile charmed me, and I asked if he wanted to see the back. I still don't know what prompted me to do this. We toured the industrial kitchen, and I pretended to know how things worked. This oven for the baguettes, that one for the bagels. When he was about to leave, I gave him the day-old pastries, frosting making a messy snow globe of the bag, and he looked at me, stared right through me as if he were really seeing me. Outside, it was starting to pour, water curtaining off the store's awning in thin sheets. He leaned against the counter—a move I would later recognize as one of his favorite shoot poses. The light was golden, dimming with the sun through the rain. He left his business card: *Lucas Hayes, Photographer, Weddings & Headshots.*

I had seen something like this happen on a reality television show I'd watched the night before, in which beautiful women flirt with ugly men, and the reactions are recorded. They all believe they have a shot.

I waited twenty minutes after he left to lock the door.

"How have you been? It's been, God, twelve years?"

How Diane recognized me was itself unbelievable—it must have been something about the cowlicks in my hair, maybe, or my profile. The fact I still hadn't grown any taller. I regretted having taken her to prom, where she must have learned enough about my features in the sheer glare of gym light to recognize me now. The coffee shop began to blur: a mosaic of browns and tans. I felt suddenly unmoored from my ability to contain my lies, to seal them from touching one another. Luke and the man continued talking at the table, and I expected at any moment for Luke to rise from his seat, take a good look at me—staring through, really seeing me—before walking into the cold, bustling streets of New York.

"I've been good, thanks," I said. I hugged her quickly. Her coat smelled strongly of dust. I turned to Luke, moved by the idea that so long as I could lump everyone into one conversation, I could manage what was said, broker the facts. Like a Vegas dealer, aware of all the aces.

"Still up in Vermont. Visiting a friend here," I said, nodding once toward the man. "What brings you to the city?"

"Oh, I'm a talent scout," she said, with a kind of *I'm a successful New Yorker* pride I could never buy. I could sense Finn perk up.

I spoke to move things along, make the unavoidable introductions. "Luke, Diane. Diane, this is my boyfriend Luke."

"Boyfriend!"

Luke, the man, and I gave her a moment to make some apology. But, being Diane—one of only three girls who auditioned for cheer squad every year and never made the team—she didn't. She had some social deficits. If I weren't the smallest alternate wrestler, and so bent on seeming straight (and pretty sure, at the time, she'd go with me), I probably wouldn't have asked her to prom.

"And who's this?" she asked, looking to the man.

"This is Finn," I said, annoyingly aware the actor forgot his own character's name. It occurred to me Luke didn't yet know exactly who Diane was, and that if I could keep it that way, I wouldn't have to guard the boundaries of my lies. I offered to help her clean the mess, and Luke and the man got back to talking—slow, mundane material about how he had recently started using conditioner (a dubious claim, but passable) and still for the life of him couldn't figure out the subway system (how embarrassing, I thought). We didn't speak while piling napkins on the floor, the liquid soaking up in dark spots, like blots in a Rorschach test.

Diane seemed as eager to end this odd episode as I was, jarred or perhaps hurt by what she must have considered my nascent homosexuality. Or maybe she really did have somewhere else to be, someone of her own to scout on the spot. Her presence was a brief blip in Finn's story, a tense, awkward hiccup. She waved on her way out the door, and Luke said, "Seems like a sweet girl."

"It's not even about trust," Luke had said. "Or just about trust. But it's, I guess—I need to know that I know who you really are."

This was when we'd gone back to his apartment after getting ice cream—that sort of test, I'd learned, to see if I was faking my lactose intolerance, which I was. The small hairs on his forearm were raised. On the television, a woman slapped a man and said something slow and deliberate, meaningful—one of those obvious, important moments, but I'd muted the sound. I felt an urgent pull toward the remote on the table; pressing the "back channel" button would reveal I had been watching *Comeback Cove*, a show in which starved-for-attention B-list celebrities compete for paltry sums by constantly throwing one another under the bus at a luxury seaside resort. Luke learning that this was my chosen entertainment would not help my case, so I changed the channel. Erasing my tracks.

"You do this thing," he told me. "You speed up, time gets fast, you overdo the detail. You jump ahead, really suddenly. And you always tell me when it's the end." He hesitated. "You know, when you lie."

"I know." I felt myself become apologetic in a way that heartened me, lending an authentic flavor of remorse to my performance. "Look," I said. "I know. You know who I am." I said this without really thinking about it. Because it's what he needed to hear, and what I wished were true. I would have given up so much for the chance to rewind to that moment in the bakery, to have said *No* when he asked if I'd baked those croissants that morning, pretending to have sore hands from kneading dough, to have been honest and forthcoming— unfailingly and gratingly myself—from the start.

"You really think that?" Luke asked.

"I know it," I said, and turned up the sound. I leaned against him on the couch, seeking that reassuring touch, but felt only his chest, the muscle of which was beginning to slide, to atrophy from whatever post-firing depression he'd lapsed into, but I didn't mind. On-screen, two actors walked dramatically away from each other without a sound.

"You feel hot," I said, putting the back of my hand to his forehead. "You should get some sleep."

Which is one way of ending an inconvenient conversation.

Luke had his answers. There was Finn in front of him. If I didn't know better, I'd think it was really him, too, that maybe this whole time I'd just come to know someone from the other side of things, imagining a man into being. But of course it wasn't true. Any more time with Finn, and Luke would had discovered the truth, left me in New York, a place I haven't been able to stand since I visited years ago. Too much gray, too much noise.

"Well," Luke said, relaxing in his seat. "Great meeting you."

"No problem," the man said, picking up the newspaper again. It was a subtle move, but it was effective. It was the work of an actor, improvising, and I thought for a moment maybe he did have what it took to make it in New York. Maybe everyone does.

"Take care of yourself," Luke added. He leaned into me and said he needed to make a call and asked if it was okay if he stepped outside for a minute. I watched him walk out the door and considered all the ways I could close Finn's story in the weeks or months to come, lock it for good like a door behind me: overdose, suicide. Car accident. His cancer. I sat down across from Finn, my left shoe sticky with the residue of Diane's coffee.

"That was kind of fun," the man said. "Thanks."

I took out a fifty-dollar bill. I'd actually gone to the ATM and withdrawn the money earlier in the week, in preparation for bribing someone into doing this. But the lifting feeling, the sense I'd emerged from something and not sunk deeper into it, was so strong I didn't care that I couldn't afford to lose the money.

"Put it under your roles: Finn," I told him. I turned away and picked lint off my coat. The crowd was clearing, and I imagined Luke outside the shop waiting for me, walking away with him, driving until the skyscrapers shrunk into a thin smog in the rearview and mountains rose on the horizon, snow falling over the hills. I imagined falling asleep next to him, my chin against the back of his neck, his pulse on my jaw.

I looked back for a moment and adjusted my collar. "But don't make it seem like some big part," I said, smiling. "Like Romeo."

Finn was right there, almost—just for a moment. He looked at me as if I had a generous bone in my body, like I wasn't just trying to save my own skin.

"Maybe more of an Iago," he said.

"Exactly," I said, pretending I knew who that was.

I walked out of the store, heard the sharp clang of the bell. Luke hugged me from behind and whispered, "I'm sorry."

I said, "Don't worry about it. He liked meeting you."

What I'd learn in the next few weeks was that there are a lot of ways to break something. Luke started seeing someone else. That was one thing I couldn't control. He told me to say hi to Finn sometime for him when he left, the screen door snapping shut behind him. I followed him out onto that small wood deck, where he apologized for doubting me. He said sorry a lot. I said, "It's fine," a lot. He walked down the stairs, his luggage thumping against each step. *Like my heart*, I thought melodramatically of those sounds at the time. Spring peepers chirped outside, the same noise I remembered from all those nights falling asleep alone, my bedroom window open next to me. And then he drove off, and that was the end.

I would replay that moment of finding Finn, watch it for the sad fun it gave me, like an episode of *Comeback Cove*, when I thought about Luke and why he left. The imagined heat and taste of the scene would wash over me like a strong mountain breeze, and there I was again: manic in a coffee shop, hundreds of miles from home, trying desperately to save the thing that mattered most by first saving myself. One day when the image of Luke was finally starting to blur—what his nose looked like, or what his favorite flavor of gum was—I went on a date with Levi, the owner of a shoe company. He was intolerably boring. He asked me some questions and we got to talking about our friends.

"Mine are all back in San Francisco," he said, biting into his burger. The red juice of the meat leaked onto his plate. He told me his friends were all nurses or cooks, which I found dreadful. Rain began to fall outside, but it was tame, a pitiful drizzle—nothing at all like that day in the bakery, patting my palms on a floury counter to suggest, when I went to shake Luke's hand, that every last thing I had said was true.

Levi watched raindrops strike the window and mentioned some obvious fact, something about an umbrella he had in his car, pop music in the background cheapening every moment.

I looked around for a photo, something to draw attention, but there was nothing interesting on the walls.

"San Fran and Boston," he added, trying to jolt the conversation alive. "And I have a few in Cambridge."

"I had some in New York," I said. I tore a straw wrapper and arranged the pieces on the table as we were that day in the city. Diane, Finn. Luke and me. "But, you know how it goes."

He looked up from his meal long enough to say, "Yeah, I do."

PUNCTURE

Blue? Blue looks sort of like a healing black," I say, filling two glasses with water in the sink.

Clark is color blind, or so he's telling me. It is Sunday, three forty-five in the morning, two weeks to the day since my mother passed, and he's bleeding on my floor, brown dots on the hardwood—which only now caught my attention.

"It's just those two: blue and red," he says, rewrapping the towel around his hand. "I can see everything else."

Clark and I met a few hours ago on the dance floor at a gay bar during Indianapolis Pride. I dropped my vodka tonic and he picked up the broken glass, then someone bumped into him—that's his embarrassing version of it. As the bartender waved everyone outside, I heard somebody say, "It's like a fucking murder scene." That was before I noticed the blood on my shorts, and before Clark refused a drive to the ER, or any medical attention. But the worst of it: How do you leave someone like that? How do you say, *Sorry, I'm partially responsible for your injury and not interested?*

"So, LA?" I say, giving his uninjured hand the water.

"It's not good," he says. "The students are so dumb."

I look at his hand. The blood has turned the tan cloth almost black.

"You're studying rocks, right?"

"Geology PhD," he corrects, as if to remind me I should be impressed by the credential. "Yeah."

Someone in the street outside my apartment yells, "Don't jump the fence. Dude, you're gonna kill yourself!" I move the trash can from my bathroom next to the couch.

"But sure, rocks," he says. "Essentially."

I remember my mother taking my siblings and me to a cavern when I was fifteen, sifting bagged dirt through a sieve, looking for gems. In her bag she found a rare ruby. The staff couldn't understand how it had even got in there, but it was worth thousands, polished to an expensive shine. I want to transfer the excitement, how a moment like that cracked open our endless petty fights and made us see each other again, so I try to explain it to Clark—the entire scene—but he interrupts when I get to the part about the rocks my mother found us in the gift shop.

"Geodes," he says, swallowing the water fast to get it out. "They're really gorgeous," he adds. I stop the story. I'm more present in that memory now than I am even here: the hot wind tapping tree branches against the window, his shoes near the door, the red print of his hand on his jeans that I don't think he's noticed yet. I rip a paper towel and lay it over a spot of blood. It expands rapidly, like a dilating pupil.

"They're really beautiful," he says.

I can tell he wants me to agree, to pin this down as the point, those beautiful rocks we found that I only care about because he's here in front of me. I'm not going to get to the part about how my sister, now backpacking alone in Brazil, tried to open hers with a hammer, or how my mother—buried hundreds of miles northeast—kept one, uncracked, in her sock drawer. A rock that might still rest there. I suddenly want to hit the conversation with a hammer, for all this talk to just shatter. "They *are* beautiful," I say. "Do you work with them?"

"They're actually not that interesting," he says.

"You're bleeding a ton."

"I'll be *fine*."

"Can you see what color this is?" I say. I lift a soaked paper towel. The light from my bedroom backlights the spot, a horror-movie red.

"It's red," he says.

"Can you *see* it, though?"

"I know it's my blood."

"So you can't see it. Jesus, you need stitches." Another drop falls from his pinky finger. "You really do."

"I'll be okay," he says. He laughs a little, trying to convince me. I bend to spray the floor with cleaner, and I briefly wonder if "okay" is different than "fine."

"It's just a temporary puncture," he says. There is a pause. "Hey," he adds. I can hear him smiling. "Do you want my number?"

Down the street, an ambulance screams.

"Do you want more water?" I ask.

"Are you okay?" He furrows his brows.

"Of course," I say. The blood smears on the wood. It doesn't lift as easily as I think it will. As I clean, I imagine myself in his classroom in California late at night, all the doors locked and windows closed, the rows of rocks and formalin-injected reptiles behind thick glass. A giant geode cracked open, a layer of dust dulling its sparkling core.

"You sure you're okay?" he says.

"Of course," I say again. I toss the paper towel in the trash, where it lands with a wet thud, and tear a new sheet. "But look at you."

RIVER IS TO OCEAN
AS _____ IS TO HEART

Ty drew a breath and dove off the far end of the pier, sliding under the skin of the cool waves. It was late May, and the water on the Cape still held a chill. This was the first time he'd taken out the buoys to cordon off the swimming area, the first time he'd done so as Assistant to the Lifeguard, a bogus community-service job he was wasting his final high school summer for. But then, as his mother had said, it was his own fault he'd had to do community service in the first place. It was his own fault he had cheated, and then lied about cheating, on a standardized exam.

"Here?" Ty yelled. His arms kneaded the dark water in wide circles. His left, wound with blue and white rope, looked ghostly beneath the surface.

On the pier, Max waved his hand forward.

A rush of wind blew Ty's hair back. If he hadn't been eager to see how he looked and felt swimming after spending the winter lifting weights in his parents' basement, he would have asked Max to set the buoys—Lifeguard Max with his protruding stomach and absent biceps. It occurred

to Ty often that Max wouldn't actually be able to save anyone. It didn't matter that they were the same age. If there
was an emergency, Ty'd be the one to race into the water,
to lift and console and check for a pulse, to place both
hands over the heart and push.

"Here?" he yelled. Max gave a thumbs-up.

The water around Ty was a pocket of eerie warmth.
Growing up, he'd imagined all sorts of things beneath him
while swimming—sharks and stingrays had been his worst
fears until he'd thought up the idea that maybe there was
no ocean floor, only a bottomless pit of water on which
he was a floating mote of dust. He released a breath and
looked up at the sun, a bright dot on the horizon. He let go
of the buoy and dropped its lead anchor, his muscles relaxing with the release. On the pier, Max was walking toward
the parking lot, the crack of his ass visible over a slouching
bathing suit.

Ty would lift himself out of the water and up the
wooden ladder, a breeze whipping him from the side. He
would walk the few miles back to his house, neglect biology homework, and fall asleep listening to the town clock
strike a new hour, like he always did. He would have done
these things if he hadn't decided instead to swim the fifty
yards to the shore, for the added exercise. Then as his foot
met the sooty detritus, it kicked something smooth and
round. Waiting for the brown cloud of sand to settle, Ty
saw it in a flash, as if dreaming: the two dark hollows of
sockets looking past him, the barely gray bone of a skull
resting like a shell on the ocean floor.

Two weeks before, Ty had been sitting at a desk in the school gymnasium, completing the first in a series of timed sections, finding the values of Xs and Ys he'd deemed totally useless since the seventh grade.

Looking back, Ty thought it must have been something about the silence, the stillness of the hot air that had given him the confidence to look up from his desk and over at Sam's paper. He had to crane his neck, faking a stretch, to see her answers. And then Ty's precalculus teacher, one of those men who only knew numbers and jokes about numbers, lifted his calculator and dropped it on the desk, snapping him back into the moment. When Ty was asked to gather his things, he hesitated. He tried to summon tears but, unable to, complained instead about his neck, and how he'd been told to stretch it, and how he knew what it looked like, and that he was sorry.

After Ty had handed in his exam, the paper was checked against Sam's, and he'd forgotten—in the rush of having gotten away with it—that he'd kept too strictly to her answers. And then he was sitting in a high-backed chair in the principal's office, with his mother on the phone, crying, her high voice audible from across the room. And then there he was, sighing on the far edge of the pier, meeting Lifeguard Max, asking him if he'd ever cheated on anything.

"There was one time, when I was in track and field," Max had said. "And I cut into the woods. I just stopped running."

"That's not cheating," Ty had said, slicking back his wet hair in the water's reflection. It almost disgusted him. "That's just giving up."

Ty didn't call out for Max right away. He stood, the water at his waist, and blinked at the bone. At first, he thought it might be plastic, a toy or a conch shell broken by the rolling surf, beaten into the shape of a skull. But it was too big—an adult's head, Ty thought. He could make out the fine lines, the faint gray cracks mottling its surface, the ridged nasal cavity, and the long row of teeth, which appeared sharper, smaller than he'd expected.

"Max! Jesus, check this out."

Ty walked slowly out of the water, careful not to disturb the silt, and through a small bed of saw grass needling his feet, onto the shore. Max turned and walked back toward him. His large orange shirt was partly tucked into his swimsuit, and only now did Ty see that he had a slight limp to his right leg, more apparent when he walked on the sand.

"This is fucked up," Ty said. He laughed as he said it, still in shock.

"What is?"

"Just walk out. Right over there." Ty pointed out at the water. "Like near that buoy. Like thirty feet."

"What is it?"

"You'll see."

"If it's something dead, just tell me. I already washed my feet off."

"It's not something dead."

The lie had come so easily, and with such conviction, that Ty almost believed it himself.

"Well, I'm going," Ty said, walking back in the water. Gulls helixed over the pier, landing on the tips of posts and docked boats. The day was quiet this late and at low tide, and the stillness lent the afternoon a hollow, gutted feel. "Come on. You have to see this."

It was either the soup kitchen, highway litter removal, or assisting the lifeguard. Those were the options, his father had said. After a pause, he'd added, "And I can't believe we're even giving you options."

The consequences were light: a two-week suspension from school, time Ty spent doing push-ups in his bedroom and showing his mother practice problems he'd done months back as proof of his improved attitude and ethic. And the part-time position assisting the lifeguard through the summer. His free time—and it really was free time, with his father working long hours at the bank and his mother often visiting priests or off at Bible study—afforded Ty other opportunities. For instance, he'd started talking to men online.

He'd found xXZachXx one night a few days into his suspension, and it was hard for Ty to chart how exactly it happened, but hours after talking in the DISCRETE chat room, his laptop heating up on his thigh in bed, he'd be-gun making plans to meet the man, who lived a half-hour drive away in Provincetown. The man's photo showed him leaning against a *No Trespassing* sign, wearing a puka shell necklace and sunglasses, cropped to show just him—from the waist up, his vaguely defined abs and thick neck—though someone else's tan hand rested on his shoulder.

When his mother came home that night, after visiting the church for one of her frequent devotion Masses, she walked into Ty's room. As he shut his laptop, she lifted a string of red rosary beads from her purse. She sat on the edge of his bed and asked him to pray with her. And he wasn't sure why, but he said yes.

Max didn't see the skull at first. He saw something else, or he must have, because he just stood there, hands on his hips, squinting down into the water. Or maybe he was looking at it the wrong way, like those mosaics Ty had seen in waiting rooms, the images snapping into place when you focused hard enough.

"It's a skull," Ty said. "Like a guy's."

Though the sky was beginning to darken and the water with it, Ty could still make it out—that white oval on the ocean floor, shifting with the waves like a mirage. He leaned over it, inching closer, and considered reaching his arm down toward that smooth, slick arch of the bone, when he heard a sudden, heavy splash behind him. The weak evening light hit the water like glass as he turned. The water rippled around him in strong rings. Max had fainted.

In the days after chatting with xXZachXx, Ty learned that his real name was Tom, that he had family near where Ty lived. He was thirty-seven. He "traditionally dated younger." He was serious and worked at a law firm. He used formal language, said "content" instead of "happy." He hadn't worked out in a year but was getting back into it, slowly. He offered to pick Ty up and take him out to dinner the next night, and Ty agreed.

There was a nervous weight in Ty's stomach in the hours leading up to meeting Tom, a feeling Ty had associated with his regular lying, that sensation of getting away with something—but what? He paced around his parents' house alone, opening windows and closing them, doing dishes, taking out the ingredients of recipes to cookies and cakes, spreading them on the marble countertop, and deciding that no, he wasn't hungry.

He sat at the dinner table, where on weekend nights he ate with his parents, looking out the window, and imagined the car slowing to park across the street, beneath the shade of the willow tree. He watched then as sparrows disappeared into the waving gray tendrils. And then, as if he'd called for it, a small silver car parked beneath it, and the crows shuddered out the top and away at once, scattering in the bleak sky.

Ty picked Max up out of the water as he'd been taught to during training—lifting with his legs, his forearms carrying the weight. If this were a rescue operation, in water off the continental shelf, Ty would have panicked, having to dive to kick and ration his breath. But the water was shallow, and Max seemed to regain some composure after being lifted to his feet. He curled Max's arm behind his neck, the cold weight of it on his shoulders. Ahead, wind bent tall grass in hard diagonals and small crabs hurried into their holes in the sand. The air was chalked with salt, touched with panic.

He brought Max to the shore, setting him down on his side. What Ty hadn't realized—and maybe it was because he never really looked at Max straight on—were his eyes, a striking pale blue, like the water Ty had seen in postcards of white sand beaches, though he didn't want to admit this even to himself as he checked for a pulse and felt it: a strong beat Ty could match with the rhythm of his own.

Tom hadn't called that evening as Ty had expected. He just arrived. The way Ty had imagined this moment the night before, restless in bed, Tom called before he parked on the side of the street—not in front of the house, as Ty was sure to tell him—to pick him up. Each hour of that afternoon waiting had passed as if a painful memory he was paying for in advance, slow and difficult to endure. He almost wished he had school, something to occupy him.

Tom parked on the side of the street under the tree, four minutes early. The man got out of the car and tilted his neck as if in a yawn. Ty could see his pale, jowled face, a round stomach that the photo had somehow hidden. He suddenly wanted to put a world of distance between himself and this man, to have avoided talking to him, even. Ty walked up the stairs to his bedroom to get a better view, but the height only offered up other flaws, like that Tom was balding, a thin circle of brown hair on his head.

Ty knew his mother wouldn't be home for several hours and that his father was gone for the night, away on business. So he lay on his bed, one ear against the pillow, and listened to the sound of his breathing as he heard the first soft knocks on the front door.

Before he kissed Max, before he'd closed his eyes and considered, really, what it would feel like—the soft cut of Max's lips on his—Ty hesitated. He knew Max had fainted. He knew there was protocol, the details of which he'd forgotten in the manic disorder, the confusion of his thoughts. Max looked dead, and his skin seemed to Ty almost blueing, turning slightly with color. Ty placed two hands on Max's chest and pressed, stopping every few seconds to check for a pulse under the jaw. A strong wind stirred the branches and the sand swirled around him. The moment felt like an unreal blur, the kind of thing he would bat away—an intrusion into a daydream. He leaned toward Max's face, waiting to feel the breath on his cheek—but nothing.

Ty let his lips align with Max's, which were dry and cold. He didn't remember how to breathe air into someone else. He didn't even know what he was doing at first. And then Max woke, or came to, coughing, and Ty pulled away from him, the sand hard in his palm. And they both stared ahead, past each other, at the thin stripe of warmth on the horizon, the wind rushing through the cattails like whispers behind them.

Ty turned over in his bed, listening for any sound of Tom outside. The knocks subsided after a few minutes, and Ty could only hear the faint clicking of the humidifier, the steady wash of a fan in the corner of his room. He sat up in his bed and walked to his desk, where the pages of an open book of practice problems whipped back and forth in the breeze.

He closed his eyes and slapped one hand against the book, stopping it on a random page. He opened them and saw analogies, those awful, useless comparisons, and picked up his pencil. Outside, there was the sound of a sputtering engine, and then its fading noise as the car drove away.

Before now, whenever he chose to sit and pretend, Ty had made a point to copy the answers from the back of his book. Normally, he did this when his mother was nearby, cleaning rooms down the hall or while letting stew sit before dinner. But tonight it was just him, and he wanted to answer just one question correctly himself. He couldn't. Instead, he recalled one of the analogies he'd taken from Sam's exam the week prior, his shivering pencil against the paper, neck tilted (or strained?). RIVER is to OCEAN, the paper read, as _____ is to HEART.

Ty remembered shading the corresponding circle, copying the answer: VEIN. He remembered the fleeting thought too: He didn't need to cheat for that question. He already knew the answer.

———

Ty tried not to remember whatever had happened in the weeks after he asked Max, quietly, if he needed help getting up off the sand, the sky clotting to a gorgeous sherbet orange behind, his bottom lip quivering. He dreamed of it some nights, though—the slippery arch of the bone against his toe, the shimmering white oval of it out on the water. The moments over Max, almost wondering if he was looking at someone dead, or dying.

After he went home that night, unable to sleep, Ty imagined himself walking silently down the stairs, out the front door, through the night thick with mosquitoes and those warm winds, beneath the glow of lampposts and toward that water. He would stand on the shore and watch for a sign of that skull, imagined seeing it lit like a lantern beneath the calm waves, but he would find nothing. He imagined himself sitting on the splintering edge of the pier, waiting for the proof to wash up near the water's edge. But there would be only the soft tapping of docked boats against the wood with the rising tide.

Max wouldn't ever look for the skull. He still didn't believe it was real, and cited his low blood pressure, mumbled something about a condition, as they spoke the next day.

"I know what I saw," Ty said. "I even *felt* it."

"Fingerprints," Max said. "Well, footprints," he corrected. "What would you even do, if you found them? Tell someone?"

The two sat at the edge of the pier, and Ty felt as if he'd

given something away, let something slip from between his hands and back into the water. He knew with upsetting certainty that Max would not ever take him seriously again; it felt unfair in a way that confused him.

Lifeguards weren't needed here. They were needed on the main beaches, those long stretches of hot tan sand, but not near the pier, and not as boats sidled boringly up next to their posts.

"You know," Max said, breaking the silence. He turned to Ty, his eyes full of confident wisdom. "You don't have to go around pretending." Ty thought he was talking about the skull, until he added, "And it's okay."

The words seemed to come out of nowhere—prompted, Ty thought, by nothing.

Ty lifted himself off the pier, flexing his shoulders back, and almost pushed Max into the water. It would have been so easy. Max was weak, and if he was a real lifeguard, Ty thought, he could at least save himself. In fact, maybe he shouldn't have lifted him from the water when he'd had the chance. As he walked off the pier and onto the searing pavement of the lot, up the hill, he tried to wash himself of what he'd just thought. He didn't hate Max. He felt the apology almost in his pulse, and remembered praying that rosary with his mother, seeking that untenable forgiveness, and began to speak a prayer aloud, just to himself, as he walked up onto the main road, toward his home, and only realized minutes later when he stepped onto the prickly welcome mat at his front door that he was walking barefoot.

At his desk, Ty took the algebra textbook from his drawer and tilted back as he often did in class, leaning at a dangerous angle. But here in his bedroom there was no one to stop him. He closed his eyes and let the fan's breeze raise the small hairs on his neck, then curl up the collar on his shirt. He tilted farther back, until he knew he was unstable, and let go of the desk.

For almost an entire minute, which he counted in slow seconds, he stayed balanced. After, he closed the book, stood, and walked to the widow. Seeing a car had parked beneath the tree, he felt a surge of fear that it might be xX-ZachXx, returning to try to meet again. But it was just a neighbor slamming the door, bags of groceries at his side. A graduation party in their backyard—yellow and pink balloons tied to a fence.

The days sped into weeks, and the weeks into months. The summer blurred like blood in the water, and Ty couldn't find the skull. He searched for it while scraping barnacles from pier posts and siphoning water out of dinghies that had sprouted leaks, but there was no evidence of its existence. Max still didn't believe the skull had ever been there. He had just felt sick that day, he told Ty one afternoon. It had been something about the air. Ty wondered if he brought the skull up as a kind of apology, a way of saying maybe it was real.

Ty started talking to other men online. Tom stopped

messaging him. Occasionally, he would see Tom's face, the lie of that photo in a small box to the right of the screen, and he would wonder what Tom had done after leaving, whether he realized the truth—that Ty had seen him and wasn't interested anymore. And then, one night as he fell asleep, it occurred to Ty that maybe this happened all the time with people like Tom—putting one image forward, forgetting the truth. Ty thought of himself, casting out years and becoming a man like that. How he might some-day wish to swim back to this exact moment. A green dot next to his face on the chat bar, his hair receded to a patchy fuzz, typing out that same opening line he used now: *Hey mister, what's up?:)*

One night in mid-July, Ty heard keys turning in the lock, his mom walk in the front door of the house. He closed his computer, turned off the fan, and listened to her voice, her side of the conversation, which was high with stress. Ty inched his bedroom door open, careful not to make noise, quieted his breathing, and turned off his light. He wasn't supposed to be home yet, but he'd left the pier early, and he waited, listening.

"He's out helping that boy in that club, the one for people who need friends."

"It *is* a good idea. He doesn't have any. And he could learn a lot from that kid, Max. The AP one."

"No, no."

After a long pause in the conversation, Ty stopped listening. He imagined Max alone on the small lip of the beach, drawing in the sand with an oar. It clicked painfully into place that he was a kind of prop friend for Max. Ty felt cheated, living a lie someone else had created for him. He thought maybe his mother had hung up the phone, before he started listening again and she added, "Right, that's what I'm saying."

"I only donate every other week. You know that."

"Don't hang up on me. Don't you do that again."

"Honest to God, Don. We both know. At best? He's going to a state school."

"We don't know if it's a habit. It might've just been the one time."

By early August, Ty had become consumed with finding the skull. He spent as much of his time in the water as possible, the skin on his legs softly rippled after hours out under the pier, as if transforming him into an amphibious creature that lived there. He wanted to tell someone about it— but who would believe him? He started leaving men fake numbers to call. He started pretending to be interested in serious dating—in marriage, even—and then stopped talking to them altogether. He gave them the address a few doors down from his home but said he was moving far away, to San Francisco or Quebec, to Stanford. A full ride, he wrote to one man, Carl, trying to keep his spelling perfect. He imagined himself as Max then. *I got lucky*, he typed. *Very lucky*.

Then it was the night before his last day of lifeguarding duties for the summer. He hadn't saved anyone. No one swam in that water anymore. He hadn't really done anything, he realized. He was in bed watching the sun set, the film of his life skipping like a broken record over that one scene: craning his neck to see Sam's paper, the sweat of his palm on the pencil, the glare of that fluorescent gym light on his unused calculator.

Ty took a large yellow flashlight from his closet. He walked out of his room and down the stairs, out the door, barefoot into the wind, leaves blowing across the house's cobblestone path and falling in the streets. He walked under the willow tree, birds scattering down in a pulse and collecting into formation before flying away. He continued until he saw the water, then out onto the pier, where Max was hunched, reining in the rope of a lobster trap someone had set illegally.

Max turned slightly and nodded toward Ty.

"What's your problem?" Ty said.

It took Max a second to respond. "I only get to pick one?"

"You really don't get it, do you?" Ty said, undoing the top button on his shirt. What he meant by this he didn't know. It seemed like the sort of thing that established a tone, that said, *Don't ask me that again.* A breeze turned up his collar. He fixed his gaze near the far buoy and tensed his calves, which he hoped had thickened with muscle since the summer before, when he'd jumped into this same spot so carelessly. He looked down between the planks of the pier and saw a thin line of his reflection. There were

dark lines under his eyes. It frustrated him that he looked
tired, a thought he knew he would lose sleep over, and envisioned the calm black ocean as an endless chat room before him, that blank space unfurled like an empty scroll
out to the horizon.

"What're you doing?" Max asked.

For a moment they both paused, and the soft blast of a
foghorn sounded. The clouds were low and gray with rain.
Ty felt the moment become heavy, baited with dumb significance, an empty mark waiting to be filled in.

"What're you doing?" Max said again, the question directed more at himself this time, dropping the line. He
looked to Ty's hand, the flashlight. Ty released a breath.
He imagined running his palms over the skull, its bone
glowing white like an answer in the darkness, feeling that
sand-tumbled smoothness, and rising in the water with it
under an arm. He could almost feel that pressure against
his ears as the water grew light, struck with a sudden ray of
sun, bubbles shooting up around him, the full beam of
light that had helped him find it.

Ty wanted to start over. There was the mess he'd made
around him, cluttering him in, and he needed to prove something, make someone believe him. The thought washed
against him like a wave, pulling in and then out—impossible,
and then clear, suddenly simple.

Ty would not find the skull. He would dive into his reflection, far and deep, toward the ocean floor, that place
where the water was cold with possibility. He would kick
down until all was black around him, the disturbed silt

tickling his skin. He would swim until he couldn't tell where he was except by how his body lifted when he paused, his limbs invisible and shrouded in darkness, that futile light of a single beam shooting through the water as he tried, finally, to see.

HUMAN RESOURCES

Anthony has this white pin on his right lapel that reads MY INTERESTS ARE: ANIMALS & POSITIVITY. Every employee has one of these pins, and everyone is required, I guess, to list two of their prominent interests. My interest, if I worked at a place like ElectronicZone, would be in how, exactly, a guy like Anthony goes from running over the neighbor's chickens with a golf cart in the sixth grade to wind up, twelve years later, with those top two favorite things, ANIMALS & POSITIVITY. That would not fit on the pin, of course, so I'd settle for something equally true, like VERY SMALL, CATLIKE DOGS. EXPENSIVE WINES. Or, if I'm being honest (a *least* favorite thing), CHEATING ON MY HUSBAND. Of course it's Anthony, who I messed around with in that broken mall photo booth, because who better to see two days before Christmas, when everyone is wearing two jackets, and the lines are backed up to the burner phones—the cheapest variety of which is in my left hand. I had no way of knowing the checkout I chose, one of the availably lit dozen, would lead me right into his view. But I'm back in my hometown of Laconia, New Hampshire, for the mercifully short window of seventy-six hours, a period I calculated during my ascent from Phoenix. Before I'd boarded the plane, my partner, Lex, had told me that "God knows this will be a good break from human resources." And now I'm looking for a reason to release my pity on Anthony. Anthony who failed home economics for starting a grease fire. I'm looking right at him, the dumb tattoo of a rose on his neck curling up from under his red and white company-issue polo. Through the distant beeping of every item past the register, some happy holiday jingle between us, I realize he isn't even going to look up at me. He won't even have the chance to see how I look now, how I got every wish I wanted. He looks in my direction, but it's like he doesn't remember. Like he knows it's me and doesn't need to say anything. Like we were never just down the street, pausing midkiss when he turned to the lens and said to no one in particular, "Does that thing even work?"

AIM FOR THE HEART

for Poppy

When Troy thought of what it might be like, falling asleep the night before, to kill that animal, he imagined a version of himself physically transformed, more solid—a strong cut of jaw, brows thick lines of concern, all his features suggesting the power it would take to stop a heart.

The next day, Troy was trailing that buck through the snow, the blood from its punctured chest now only faintly visible in the slush. Neil walked alongside the animal— examining the watery film of its eye, pulling back to observe the twitching tail. This, Troy knew, is what happened when you lied in passing about being an *avid hunter*. After you made a promise to show your boyfriend how hunting *works*. You opened that box containing your father's old gun and drove your pickup with the only man you have ever loved down a mud-rutted road into untraveled backwoods. You walked slowly around the pines, listening with an air of practice for the sound of an animal you knew you'd never find. And then a young buck wandered lazily into your path. You knelt slowly, acting the part, and tried to miss, prayed to miss. And despite what Troy had read about how easily deer scare, how scarce the chance of even a sighting in Maine mid-February, the lone buck had turned its head as if in invitation, its ears pivoting toward the noise of his boot crunching the snow. He aimed slightly to the left and pulled the trigger. The sound startled the deer directly into the bullet's path, and it fell onto its side, tossing up a celebratory white plume of powder.

And now, here he was: rattled by a deep cold, followed by a man who couldn't kill an ant without squirming, dragging a deer by the antlers a quarter mile back to his pickup, where he'd swaddle the body in a blue tarp normally reserved for summer mulching.

It didn't occur to Troy until after they'd reached the road that he could have found some reason not to take the buck. *Not regulation* or *Could be diseased—see this?* And then he'd point to some questionable feature: a dirtied coat, perhaps something as easily missed (that could only be caught by an expert hunter) as the color of its eye. Something Neil would believe. But even that would have been difficult, he realized, as he struggled to lift the body into the bed of the pickup. Bullet wound aside, the creature was all perfect cream coat and short, sleek hair. Troy hoped that at any moment the deer might kick free of his grasp and dart off, back into the wilderness, so that they could both continue on living.

When Troy was in middle school, he'd been pulled from homeroom and questioned by the vice principal; his close friend Iffer had shot himself that morning with his grand-father's handgun, barely missing his heart—miraculously, the surgeon claimed—causing significant damage only to his left lung. The school and his family were looking for reasons. If-fer was found when his mother, who'd forgotten her library card, returned to see him bleeding out into the shower—a de-tail Troy learned through a rumor that had traveled around the school faster than a virus. The way she told it, there wasn't blood—just heaving and painful wheezing. A pipe had burst when the bullet met the wall, she had made a point to men-tion. As if to relocate the damage in the story. He wondered whether Iffer's mother actually thought that anyone believed this—that thank God they had survived this violent hiccup in their otherwise calm, normal lives. Or if maybe she believed it herself: that something had broken and mended swiftly, the way a lizard can regrow a severed tail in days. He suspected the damage that water had done gave her a way out of Iffer's story, and that she was grateful for it.

"Has Iffer ever done anything that's made you uncom-fortable?" the vice principal asked. He folded his hands on his lap and waited.

Once, several weeks prior, Iffer had reached for Troy's hand at the middle school dance. Troy didn't pull away when Iffer had wrapped his fingers around his palm, and the two stood silent in the darkest corner of the gym, an industrial fan washing them with aggressive cold. The next day, he'd said to Iffer, *Sorry, whatever that was.*

Yeah, Iffer had agreed.

"No," Troy said, but the man was already writing on his pad like he knew better.

———

Troy drove off that road rutted by frozen mud, and turned onto the interstate en route to Neil's for the night. As he made the turn, he noticed in the rearview that antlers shining with frost poked out of the bed of the pickup, clinking against the cold metal with each lurch of the truck. He remembered something about needing a license to hunt as the police siren sounded behind him.

Troy pulled carefully over, and the officer approached the car. Troy could see in his rearview the man's narrow face, the inflamed red bulb of his nose, his eyes poring over the animal. It was not an especially big deer—a young buck, Troy suspected. He decided that, if prompted, he would call it such to avoid appearing unsure.

The man asked to see Troy's license and registration. He hadn't turned from examining the deer. Neil handed Troy the papers.

"Troublemaker," Neil said, smiling.

"Always," Troy said. Troy did have plans for the buck, though they were shapeless plans—a vague idea of having it stuffed or preserved, a trophy. Something about having killed the buck made him feel like he hadn't lied to begin with, that he'd just had some premonition, some prescient sense. Neil had believed Troy so easily when he'd mentioned his hunting habit months ago. He sometimes thought he looked the part himself: slight gut, thick neck, a strong frame that held the attention of football and hockey coaches through high school. Troy decided to avoid hunting duck with Neil due to the sheer number of birds he imagined in the area—surely deer would be harder to come by, he'd thought.

But now, as the officer approached his window, Troy felt the quietly exhilarating rush of having trapped himself in a lie from which it was likely he could not emerge without his own scar.

On only a few occasions had Troy ever been found out. Once, during college, drunk at midnight on the roof of the Deaf Studies building, he divulged what he'd claimed was his life story to a group of other flannel-wearing, guitar-playing students he'd met just hours before. In it, he had a sister, Lauren, who was in law school and had an enormous mole on her nose. There were his parents, a doctor and nurse as they were, but in this version they were both under lawsuit for malpractice. And the people seemed to believe him. They seemed eager to accept whatever he put forth. So he kept talking, kept offering these gifts of fabricated strangeness. It was almost generous, he remembered thinking. He was giving these people stories they could tell for the rest of their lives.

At one point, under the clear black sky, a breeze moving over the building, Troy considered mentioning Iffer. But he felt Iffer's place among the lies would be inappropriate, as if the story in its truth couldn't touch the serrated, fragile edges of Lauren and the time he'd gone "cow-tipping" and his family in all their false ruin. Eventually, Troy told a story about how Lauren once tried to remove a friend's mole with his father's practice scalpel, not realizing that very same friend had arrived on the roof while he was speaking, and he found himself deflating with the weight of the truth, uncovered if only to one person. He walked back to his dorm room and wrote on a notepad the words *Stop lying* over and over, before resting his head on his forearm, and falling asleep. When he woke, the ink from those words was smeared on his forearm.

Eventually, it always became too much effort to chart the paths of his lies, and Troy would move from person to person, let his imagined selves peel away like shed skin. He was a terrible student and spent only a handful of his evenings in the library (where he imagined Iffer did the same with much more discipline), reading on business and economics, fascinated by the futility of it all, how he could sense the knowledge practically expiring as he read. Those facts slipping away, turning into something else. He often found himself looking up in study carrels, bored by the material, and tending to his ever-evolving image, the mirage of himself growing fainter and fainter before disappearing entirely. Who knew what of him? How many hims existed out there, in others' minds? In his?

The lies had unfurled quickly, but, Troy knew, such was their nature: Each one had loose strings. It was just a matter of cutting those frayed bits short to keep others from taking note and pulling on one, unraveling it like a handmade sweater. The officer asked to see Troy's hunting registration. He claimed he forgot it, and when asked how long he'd been hunting, Troy said ten years. He immediately regretted saying "ten"; the cleanness of a decade felt too fake to be believable.

"Have an expired copy?"

"Should, let me check." Neil flipped through the glove box. There was, of course, no expired license.

"Guess not." The officer handed Troy a ticket and said something as the window slid up. *What?* Troy mouthed.

"A beauty," the man said. He knocked on the side of the pickup and nodded toward the animal, which, Troy noticed, was now completely visible, the officer having peeled away the folds of the tarp. Troy pulled back onto the road. One tire fell into a deep frozen gouge, jerking the truck along its path where those before him had driven.

"I thought you'd only been hunting for six years," Neil said. "Since the promotion."

"Oh," Troy said.

Troy waited for Neil to continue, but he said nothing. "Well," Troy explained, "I've heard about the new guys getting harsher fines."

Coloring the past was the most important thing in lying, Troy had learned. Tell someone you've killed a deer and they'll wonder why, how. Tell someone you've hunted on and off since getting a job managing accountants, and they'll think they know who you are.

Neil appeared to accept the response. Troy turned up the incline to Neil's home, a cabin outfitted to seem a house. Troy could always sense that Neil was nervous about having him over—he didn't come from a wealthy family and didn't make much as a baker. Troy knew this and always made a point of complimenting some feature of the space. Today it was the birch trees, white and stiff in the breeze, ghostly pillars in the night.

"Thanks," Neil said. He turned his head down, sensing pity. But Troy always meant it, whatever he complimented. He really did.

Iffer sat in the back of the classroom in the weeks following his hospitalization, and Troy was assigned as his sort of helper. During lunch, Troy sat with Iffer and, later, helped wheel him between classes. The doctors and parents emphasized the importance of rest, the power of the body to heal itself. Troy was told not to encourage Iffer to get out of his wheelchair even though he technically could walk, could probably run, if he wanted to, and only occasionally had trouble breathing. It was, he remembered thinking, as if Iffer were a deflated version of himself. Not just physically—his body slumped in an effortless curve—but in another way; some distinct sadness had settled on him. The two began to fall away from each other: Troy to a junior varsity lacrosse team and Iffer to the chess club, his thick curls of hair draped over the board, thinking or perhaps avoiding thought, moving a king into its corner for the checkmate.

By June, Iffer's lung had become deeply infected, and a complex series of procedures saved his life but not without the cost of great damage to the organ. In freshman year of high school, he wheeled through the halls, unable to attend classes on the third floor, and remade himself as a bookish, tired boy.

When Troy would pass Iffer on his way to calculus, he'd occasionally remember that hand in his, that night in the gym, the groups of kids too busy to notice the two of them, paralyzed by a friendship they couldn't understand. But Troy would always turn away or look past, not sure what he was expecting.

That night, Troy and Neil watched breaking footage of an airplane that had crashed while attempting to land in San Francisco. A wing of the plane was severed, strewn along the runway in splintered piles, and its exterior held a dark char. Outside, the deer remained slumped in the bed of the pickup—which was fine, Troy told Neil, due to the cold. Was it fine? he wondered, just to himself. He did not want to know. The television screen cast a faint fluorescent hue through the window onto the truck, shading the animal in soft white tones in the dark.

"Ever been to San Fran?" Neil asked.

"No," Troy said. He'd avoided that city, actually: too many gay people, he thought. How could one have a lasting relationship with so many options, so much temptation? He knew this was an inappropriate thought, or somehow testament to his own insecurity.

"Those runways are scary," Neil said. "Drop right off into the water."

On the screen, medics unfolded orange gurneys, and

the shot zoomed out to show the black dot of the wreck flanked by endless ocean.

"I feel like people there are, I don't know. I feel like everyone there is really gay."

Neil cocked his head. "Sorry?"

"Sorry, that was rude."

"I mean, there are a lot of gay people there."

"Right."

"But I don't think that's a fair thing to say. That they're *really* gay." Neil was quick to get upset and quick to show it. Troy appreciated that about Neil: his inability to hide what he felt, to withhold. Still, his defensive reply seemed, ironically Troy thought given the context, a little much.

"You're right," Troy said, wanting to end the moment. "Sorry." Just to himself, he thought: *Everyone there is really gay.*

The running scroll on the bottom of the screen read: THREE DEAD, THIRTY-FOUR IN CRITICAL CONDITION. Flights to and from the airport had stopped. Above the wreck, the sky was a bright candy blue, and hot-air balloons rose from the ground in small, slow groups. Troy tried to imagine himself there with Neil, but, unable to, envisioned instead the moment of the crash: the first trembling of the cabin, the short glissando screams, the sudden weightlessness and dive, yellow plastic masks tipped down from their compartments.

Troy reached to hold Neil's hand, but the timing felt wrong. He folded his hands in his lap and watched.

———

Somewhere, Troy knew, Iffer was still alive. The news of Iffer's death or returned illness surely would've reached him. There was no way to know, but then, no—perhaps he did know. Troy's last memory of Iffer was at prom, where he saw Iffer as if those painful years had never happened, a healthy skin seemed to have grown over them; Iffer had turned into a tall, slender, meticulously dressed guy after outgrowing the wheelchair sophomore year, giving the seamless illusion that he knew who he was. He carried an inhaler and held himself in a slight, constant slouch—but he was becoming well again. Iffer danced with his hands in fists, neon lights pulsating in the air behind him. Easily mistaken, from across the room, as someone, anyone else.

As the evening drew to a close, most parents arrived to pick up their kids, and Troy and Iffer remained on the inn's patio afterward, waiting. Several juniors mingled around a table lit by large red candles, and the air smelled romantically of summer in Maine, purple lilac and the rising tide. Troy wandered toward Iffer, who leaned against a small fence.

He looked tired. His corsage had lost most of its pink petals, but his tuxedo seemed freshly pressed, as if he'd only just arrived.

"Hey," Iffer said, noticing Troy. "How's it going?"

"It's going." Troy leaned back on a table, taking in the scene. He wanted to feel attractive to Iffer, but then, he'd never felt he had to try until now. It was one of those rare moments when it was permitted to speak in terms of lives and goals and dreams, and Troy was coming down from the high of discussing his plans to run a small business and move far away. The two briefly talked about college, their insufferable parents, pets that had passed away since Troy and Iffer had lost touch. The others on the patio left. They were finally alone, again.

"That was a weird thing," Iffer said, presumably talking about the incident. He leaned his head back and closed his eyes. "I used to be so angsty." He smiled, coughing one syllable of a laugh. He was avoiding eye contact, or Troy wasn't inviting it.

"It happens," Troy said. He regretted those words even as he spoke them. Shooting yourself in the lung doesn't just *happen*, he thought.

But this was all Troy would receive from Iffer, the closest thing to an explanation he'd ever get. Troy's father pulled up, wheels grinding gravel and turning into the lot. Troy hugged Iffer before walking away. "Take care," he said as he reached to shake Iffer's large, warm hand. His father honked the horn once, and then Troy was driving home, taking extra care himself for his permit test days later, adjusting the air-conditioning toward his blushing face, wondering if he would ever see Iffer again and deciding that, no, he likely wouldn't.

When Troy woke on the couch, the television was still on. Sixteen fatalities, eleven in critical care. The plane had been bombed; suspects were in custody. He wondered why he hadn't thought of it the night before. There had been obvious signs, the exposed cabin, the charred perimeter of a gaping hole in its hull.

Troy looked at Neil and felt a shiver of delusional dread, as he often did before he left and had with many men—that this might be the last time he ever saw him. He playfully slapped Neil's thigh, and Neil twitched reflexively at the touch, then moaned and turned away.

"Hey," Troy said softly. "I've gotta run." Neil moaned again. "I'll see you later." Another moan.

Troy walked outside, taking care to close the door gently to avoid waking Neil. The deer was stuck in place, a frozen thing paralyzed in the act of dying, a body released from struggle. He looked it in the eye, that big, mournful pupil. The bullet wound was smaller than he'd expected, almost unassuming. How had it died so fast? He jerked open the frozen door and started the car, drove to a small building where local hunters had their animals stuffed— this he knew from a shameful one-night stand years earlier with a man whose brother worked at the shop.

When he arrived, he led the man to his pickup. The man whistled at the sight. "Haven't seen antlers like these in a while," he said.

Troy sensed the man's need to discuss the process—the kind of gun he'd chosen to take out on that fresh field of snow, where his boot prints left that romantic, intertwining trail with Neil's, and the things he'd hide from his story, like the feminine little "um" that escaped his lips when the deer lifted one front leg at the hit, then fell over. There was the feeling that escaped Troy, like a bullet exiting his heart, that for the first time he had proven his masculinity, and that there was no possible way that feeling could last. That what he had really shot was his only chance with Neil. He wanted to tell the man, unprompted, that it wasn't him! That of course he had not done this.

"Pose preference?" the man asked. He laughed a bit at his alliteration; Troy imagined he thought himself clever. He led Troy inside and pointed to model deer in a small showroom: a doe lying curled on the ground, young deer in imitation of their first awkward steps, a buck with its head fiercely turned. He asked to have the deer standing with a front leg lifted, its head down. A strange request, he knew, but he wanted a pose that seemed characteristically him, and he figured something that couldn't see but thought it knew where it was going would be fitting. He told the man he'd come back for the deer in several nights and left. A thin coat of frozen fur remained in the bed of the car after the animal was peeled off—a reminder.

When he went to pick up the deer days later, the man greeted him with a toothy smile. Troy noticed he held something in his hand, and behind him stood the deer with its slack neck, its closed eyes. It looked as if it were grazing, in repose, nothing at all like what Troy had imagined. The man opened his palm. "Perfect aim," he said. The silver shell of the bullet in his hand flashed gold with sunlight. "Right for the heart."

The rest of the week, Troy avoided Neil's calls. He turned off even the far lights down his driveway at night as if anticipating Neil's arrival, his pleading to understand. What

Troy had come to realize took shape in the memory of being handed that shining bullet: He was getting too good. The skill had not only become habit, it had become an intractable part of him. The boldest lies were these attempts to convince himself that this wasn't true; they seemed to reflect indefinitely like an image in opposing mirrors—artifice of artifice.

Troy woke next to the man who had come to fill Neil's spot in his bed. He had come over hours earlier, tracking snow around his kitchen floor, and remarked on Troy's rugged appearance, the squareness of Troy's jaw, which Troy had always doubted whenever he couldn't see it. The compliment had endeared Troy into asking him to stay the night.

After a few moments of listening to the man's calming breaths as he fell deeper and deeper into his sleep, Troy heard one gunshot outside, followed by another. He rose quickly enough to hear the rustle and snap of disturbed brush as several deer sprinted across his lawn, jumping gracefully off into the woods around his home. The next night, anticipating another pop of shells, he thought of that trespassing hunter, someone like him—cold and waiting, with everything to prove. How he might describe it, if that stranger were still next to him, or maybe to Neil, or even to Iffer, were his chest rising and falling as he'd memorized it from all those years ago: one young doe shot through the shoulder, an awkward gait to its manic run. And as Troy closed his eyes to sleep, no matter how he tried to chase it, the deer would always just barely get away.

AUDITION

Joe or Joel, whatever his name is, takes me to the roof of his LA apartment, where a small pool sends bright waves of light onto the walls and perfumes the hot August night with a chloric bite. This is date one and drink six—pretty sure about the six—of a kind of strawberry concoction that should have been drink one (the first was the cheap vodka at Simon's place before I ditched him). The city shines holographic right before us, and I feel his hand on my thigh as I throw my head back to see the stars. Every time I view the city like this, from above, it saddens me—it is everything before me I cannot have because I am not yet a good enough actor. Looking up at the stars, clear and bright like ornaments, I think, *I can't appreciate these.*

"What can't you appreciate?" Joe or Joel says, and I realize that instead of thinking the words, I had said them.

"The stars," I say in a tone that I hope communicates my desire to end that discussion. I shift my leg and his hand slides off.

"They're just dying light," he says, and I sense him lurch

his head back in the same way I had just done. Everyone knows this fact about stars; I'm offended he thinks I don't. I feel a rush of the word I want to say: "whatever." Joe or Joel is willing to agree with anything I say and do anything I tell him—he's that grateful to be around me. That's another thing I should appreciate. Instead it makes me feel sorry for him.

This on the heels of a two-year relationship with a body-builder named Chad who co-owned an organic grocery store back in Phoenix, managed the produce section with the tight-ship discipline of someone whose moods depended upon his ability to deadlift twice his weight, and frequently hit me during sex. I can call that abuse now, almost two months out. It feels heavy, the memory of it. I remind myself—*that's because it is*.

"The stars look the same as the city," I say flatly.

"And the pool," he says.

"Not really." The alcohol emboldens me to say whatever I feel, but my feelings change immediately, and so I regret almost the entire wake of what I do.

Back in May, I had asked Chad if he thought I had celebrity potential. He had been re-sorting the pomegranates into a pyramid, and I had stopped in to visit him late one night after ditching my friends.

"Not really," was his response.

In the next scene I arrive at my friend's apartment in LA. Five a.m.

"It's such a beautiful night," Joe or Joel says. He looks at me with all he's got, infusing the air with romance, but it's just another view to me.

When I first met Chad, we walked the produce section as he taught me the difference between kales. *What is this one called?* I might have said, holding up a thorny orange melon. There is nothing sexy about the way he would look at me. It would be the same stare of blunt desire, one-way want, and when it comes at you, you have to dodge it.

These days I hold kindness up like a strange fruit.

"I see what you're saying," I tell Joe or Joel. "About the pool."

I take a sip of the drink. Strawberry pulp races up the straw and clogs it. I can feel that he wants to kiss me right now, and when I look over at him I realize I'm right. I think, *What the hell am I going to do?* And then I hope—I just hope—that I didn't say that too.

HOW TO LIVE YOUR BEST LIFE

The wind that night was stung cold with luck, that envelope damp with sweat in Kyle's hand again. Here he was outside after midnight, threatening himself to mail it. He had every reason not to—a thought easily displaced by the shine of every reason he had to. The streets were dangerous this time of night. Days ago a nearby building had gone up in a planned flame, that faint smell of smoke drifting in through the crack beneath his front door. People were finally getting angry. Kyle was among them. He placed the envelope in the box and lifted its red flag.

He tilted his head toward the sky and tried to make out constellations, but he couldn't pair the stars together, couldn't imagine them into a shape. He waited there for minutes, taking in the night, until a light flicked on in the apartment, a single room in which Jerry and Chloe—his partner and daughter—slept on separate couches. It was probably another one of Chloe's nightmares. They had become more frequent. She needed medication for them, but it didn't help, and then it wasn't affordable, and now Kyle held her until she fell asleep. It actually worked, and often he didn't rest, just sat and thought, her head on his thigh, blond hair spread like the blossom of a great flower.

He didn't realize how cold the night was until he shut the door behind him.

Months before, Kyle and Jerry sat down together, finally.

"Jerry," Kyle said, "the thing is, we can't even afford two more months' rent."

Jerry folded his hands beneath his chin, elbows resting on the table. It would have been one of his drag poses, a vogue moment, if he weren't so concerned.

"I'm not doing more shows."

"Okay." Kyle lowered his voice, worried he might wake Chloe, who had been asleep for hours.

"We could lease," Kyle added.

"Absolutely not."

"The Smiths were an isolated case."

"No one knows that." There was a pause. Kyle got the sense Jerry felt like he was in a movie, and managed his anxiety in the moment by indulging these feelings, whenever they arose. "Tell me people aren't looking for handouts, Kyle. Tell me people in this town don't want something for nothing."

An almost admirable level of drama. It was true, though, Kyle knew. The city of X had a way of keeping people where they were. It was, after all, where the nation's homeless, the hugely indebted, the failing masses had been brought.

"We could sell some stuff, clear out."

Jerry's expression, a disgusted squint, read, *No.*

"Okay, then. Not that."

Neither one spoke for minutes, and Kyle could hear several stray dogs take up their coarse howling in the dusk. Kyle noticed their cries seemed to come from multiple directions at once, and he wondered how they managed it, or whether their overlapping noise was coincidence. "I'm going to bed," Jerry finally said, obviously just to himself.

That night, as Kyle lay in bed, he considered what he'd done to keep Jerry happy, the things he'd stolen now taking up residence on walls and tables throughout the house. The time that had been freed up to do this was the benefit of being unemployed, if there was one. Kyle ducked into other houses and returned with candles, mats, expensive plates and vases. The first time he'd brought himself to steal, he'd chosen a candelabra holding two unused sticks of yellow wax. He placed it on the kitchen table, unsure how he'd justify it to Jerry when he returned home. And when Jerry saw it, he smiled. "This is cute," he said, lifting it off the table. To Kyle's relief, no explanation was asked for, and none was ever given. Chloe must have assumed Jerry could afford these things; she never mentioned them either.

Kyle turned on his pillow, folding over him the recent steal of a knitted red blanket, and fell asleep.

The next morning, he woke to a note under his door. He knew the handwriting, the pink ink, was Chloe's as he bent to pick up the scrap of paper. The cursive read: *Sorry. Nightmares again.*

Kyle walked down the stairs and noticed her asleep on the couch. He wanted to sit next to her, to thank her, to let her know what he knew to be a lie. It would be okay. It was kind of her to write the note, and he was sorry she had lost sleep—sorrier that she'd heard them fighting at all. Instead, he adjusted the blanket where it had fallen to the ground so that it covered her.

Through the window, snow was falling—lightly, barely. And when he opened the door, there it was, a paper hex on his front step: the silver-rimmed envelope, sealed with a thick dot of brilliant gold wax.

The letter must have arrived early that Saturday morning. Kyle didn't know as he leaned down that the silver notes were being picked up all around town, off porch steps and inside snow-dusted mailboxes throughout X. He didn't know what exactly the letter was for, even after breaking the seal and sitting down to his morning coffee, closing the door gently to avoid waking Jerry and Chloe, who were still asleep. *How to Live Your Best Life*, the paper read in gold type. From one angle the message appeared welcoming, warm, and from the other, distant and cold like the bills he'd been paying and expecting and tried not to think about. There was a date given, a time he didn't pay attention to. *How to Live Your Best Life*. Kyle released a breath. It sounded like a scam.

But then, in the weeks that followed, he learned it wasn't a scam. It was a game. People started playing, and between seven and eight on Saturday nights, the whole town—the whole nation, really—began to stay indoors, watching people learn how much families in X knew about what one another truly wanted, if they knew how they'd choose to live their best lives. The payoff was a new life somewhere else, a quarter-million-dollar sum for each participant, a way to erase the debt and dirt, the cheap memory of living in X.

And the drawback, written in typical black type near the bottom of the page: the potential to be put to death on live television.

"It's disgusting is what it is," Jerry said, looking at the letter. "A joke. Is this a joke?"

Jerry waved the paper like a cheap fan. He was on his way to perform that Saturday night, and his makeup, the slick brown wave of his wig, gave him a fierce confidence.

"Looks real," Kyle said.

"Lots of things look real." Jerry squinted to see the print. "These lashes, for instance."

"The neighbors got one too. They came over to check."

"Well, I won't be watching."

Kyle handed Jerry his heels.

"No," Jerry said, setting the paper on the table. "The green ones."

Kyle stole only during the day. He would ring doorbells and wait for minutes. If someone answered, he pretended to have the wrong address. There were so many homes in X, but none of them were homes—not really. They were apartments, fractured living spaces, often cluttered with items about to be pawned.

This was a solution, Kyle thought. Jerry noticed the things he stole, even complimented them. Regarding a throw rug Kyle had placed in front of the bathroom door, he once said, "Did you get this? It's nice," and Kyle had said, "Yeah," and that was it.

Another time, walking back from a steal, he heard Chloe's voice calling after him. He'd lifted several bright towels and carried them on a side road, putting space between himself and the small apartment from which he'd taken them. He wasn't sure why Chloe was out, but he flung the towels over the fence just before she saw him, ran into his arms, the sunlight hot on his face like a spotlight.

Today, Jerry had finally noticed a pair of small glass doves Kyle had taken from a couple several units away. The birds rested, singing, on a small wooden mantel near the bed. Jerry lifted them and put them back down, inspecting for the signature of a brand. He didn't say a word.

The homeless were the first to go on air.

It had happened fast: Only weeks after the invitations were received, the production was going, held in a studio miles away in downtown X. It was hard for Kyle to tell if the people had volunteered or if they were somehow forced onto the show. He refused to watch at first, and Jerry was typically busy doing drag shows at the time, which were already losing money to people opting to stay in and watch the new show.

Instead, Kyle looked at the thin envelope on the table, trying to consider it as an invitation, not a death sentence. It felt impossible. He folded and unfolded the paper, checking and rechecking the words, which, though he hadn't realized it, he'd already memorized.

With Chloe asleep and Jerry gone, he decided to watch just the opening credits of the show. He felt a sense of sudden duty, as if these people, whoever they were, might need him. But then, on the set—a great marquee of flashing yellow lights and slick black glass—he saw the face of a man he thought he'd passed on the street while walking to the bank, one of those times he'd needed another loan. The man's wispy gray beard and hefty figure were backlit with strong white light, and two others stood in glass cases far behind him. The written words crossed the screen, appearing letter by letter: *How to Live Your Best Life*.

Kyle had to force his body to take in air. The springs in the couch seemed to press against him the entire hour. Between him and the monitor were only paralyzed motes of dust in the air, weakly illuminated by the evening light. When the final question was asked, the man was shivering— the camera didn't stray from close-up, and his whole body shook.

By the time the confetti had fallen, the quarter-million-dollar amount announced and announced, the man had fainted, and his siblings, released from their glass boxes, kneeled beside him, brushing the green, yellow, red paper from his beard, his eyes, remembering all the while to smile.

———

"Help me," were Chloe's words. When she woke at night, plagued by nightmares, that was what she screamed. There was something too pointed, too clear about it, Kyle thought. Years ago, when she first started having the dreams, it was those words that had made Kyle and Jerry recognize that Chloe was special. She knew how to communicate, how to help and how to ask for help, in the manner of an adult. Sometimes Kyle had to remind himself that she was a child.

The routine went like this. Kyle would pour Chloe a glass of milk and knock on her door before walking in to keep from frightening her. She would sit up, her eyes shut, breathing hard. He would stay at the edge of the bed and wait for her to move next to him, where she would lean against his arm and fall asleep. Sometimes she explained her dreams, what she'd seen. One night, she had grown painful wings but hadn't been able to fly. Or she was trapped in a stone maze with no exit.

"I was drowning," she said tonight. "Way out in the ocean."

Without thinking, Kyle whispered, "Remember? I taught you how to swim."

"It's a gym membership," Jerry said. "The manager got it for me. I have to go."

"You don't," Kyle said. He could sense Jerry wanting to stand from the table, to walk away, and added, "And it could be okay. No one's even died yet."

"Yet." Jerry paused. "And I have to go. It was free and it'll help me lose this." Jerry pinched the imagined weight in his midsection. He was thin, thinner than Kyle, and had made the recent habit of pretending things weren't what they were.

"Think about it—the death thing is just a ploy. Three months—no one's lost." Kyle paused.

"I could probably use a new comb," Jerry said before walking away.

Kyle had met Jerry at one of his performances. There was the dimming of lights and the sonic beat of a new number and then there he was: fierce, aloof, taking and throwing everyone's money on the floor. Kyle had stood and walked up to him, offered a dollar between two fingers. And later in the night, as Kyle waited at the coat check, back when he could afford the coat check, Jerry had found him. "Oh thank God," he'd told Kyle, short of breath. "You're still here." He handed Kyle the bill, which still held its crease from earlier in the night. On its edge, Jerry had written his number and the words *We should probably get coffee.* A lipstick kiss covered Washington's face. A little much, Kyle had thought, but as he later learned, that was Jerry.

And then they did get coffee, which is when Kyle learned that Jerry got his drag start after having to use his sister's makeup to cover the large scar where his ex had once thrown a plate, puckering the skin just under his eye. Jerry liked the way he felt no one knew this about him when he performed. "Just a little extra concealer" he'd said. A week later, Kyle had helped him gently remove the foundation after a show and had seen it, the scars where those sutures had been. The tenderness of the moment brought up in him a care that felt like love. One day, Jerry brought over a hand mirror and left it on the table. And the next he was walking upstairs saying, "Look, I'm going. Let Chloe stay up a bit."

Kyle walked out of his apartment at midnight, holding the envelope. He had stopped on the cement steps leading to his door, smiling, letting his white exhalations rise hopefully in the cool night. The moon seemed brighter than usual, he noticed, like a winking eye. This was a solution.

Kyle checked to make sure the envelope still rested in the mailbox and walked back inside. He didn't realize how cold it was until he'd shut the door behind him.

There were things Kyle hadn't known. He was, for example, under the impression no one would actually die on the show.

Usually, he watched alone. But tonight he watched with Jerry, who hadn't been called in—the show was losing the club money. Jerry had prepared, though—his purple eyeshadow was smeared, his short brown hair hot and flat against his head from the lace front, which he hung on the coat hook behind the front door.

The show started as it always did. A young couple from somewhere in downtown X were trying their hand. There was only the young man in the glass box, which was attached to the set itself, a thick gray tube connecting from somewhere above the stage to the glass. He stood with his hands on his hips, determined.

Kyle would return to the memory of what happened next, float it in his mind each night—an awful, unreal blur. The man answered each question incorrectly. He was prompt with every response, as if worried his partner would take offense to a slow answer. The red X appeared above him with each reply. The audience grew silent. Kyle's hands moved from his hips to his hair, worrying through it. He couldn't recall what happened before the moment the golden mist was released into the box, filling it in a rich plastic light. And then the television went black and the skull appeared slowly, softened from gray to stark white, into an image. The crossbones appeared in a perfect X below it.

"Fuck," Kyle said. He stood and walked to the kitchen. "Fuck," he yelled again. Chloe could hear him, he knew, but then, she probably wasn't asleep.

"Wow," Jerry whispered in the other room. His silence meant he was talking about the show.

Kyle leaned against the sink, both hands steadied on the cold counter. His saliva began to sour, and he sensed the feeling of both sinking and rising in his stomach. The room didn't spin, and nothing moved. Everything was terribly still.

Jerry stayed in the other room, but his voice carried clearly, cut through the mist of Kyle's panic.

"What, Kyle?"

Outside, the stray dogs barked again. Their cries sounded like firing guns. Kyle's hand touched the edge of a plate. He wanted to throw it.

———

The letter showed up early on a warm Thursday. Punishment.

Kyle opened the note at the mailbox. Weeds had started to take the small lawn, and in the corner, near his neighbor's yard, a profuse cluster of daffodils had started to raise their green fingers from the ground. His attention turned to the paper. He unfolded it, snapped it open. The first word he saw beneath the logo was "Congratulations!"

One of his neighbors walked out to her mailbox—someone he hadn't yet stolen from—and he wished to trade places with her, to pawn the note off somehow. But what *if* they won? What then would be done with the knowledge Kyle was willing to risk Jerry and Chloe for a better life? They'd always know that he had sold them out, or at least been willing to. How did he ever tip the scales back, or think he someday could?

His best life. Not his best life, he thought. There was no living that now.

Kyle waved to her and closed the mailbox. He spent the rest of the afternoon alternating between trying to figure out how to explain to Jerry that in a few weeks they would all be packing up for their new life somewhere else, and the thought that perhaps he could steal something enormous in apology. He planned how he would deliver the news to Jerry: He could leave his job, stop performing for people living their comfortable lives, watch Chloe become the brilliant girl she truly was, away from the smog, the soot, the bloodred sunsets of X.

—————

Jerry walked out of the house, halfway through putting on foundation, and returned hours later, walking back in like a storm. He told Chloe, and she cried quietly, living the nightmare of reality. Noise faded. Kyle sat in the kitchen, his thumb tracing the glimmering edge of the letter, trying to believe, to make sense of it all.

Kyle's neighbors, a couple new to X from outside the city, invited them over for dinner a month after selection. There was the mutual benefit: The neighbors could hear about the process, the anxiety, and Kyle's family could get a free meal. He'd stolen from the same apartment before the two had moved in and couldn't shake the memory of ducking in, the cold glass of the snow globe in his hand, and rushing out, tossing it in one hand on his walk back.

"We'd never go to one of the viewings," Leila said, passing a bowl of steamed broccoli. "Exciting, sure, but—"

Kyle cut into the chicken. The knife made a short yelp against the plate.

"I think it's about the possibility more than the thing itself," Leila's husband said. Everyone perked at his voice— no one expected him to speak about the show, or even at all. He worked as a newscaster. His business had been devastated by the popularity of the show. It was what Kyle imagined drove them into X in the first place.

"I think that's right," Jerry said. He paused, chewing.

"Like with stripteases. People don't want to see everything, just enough."

"Some people want to see everything," Chloe said. Attention shifted to her as she reached for a roll. "Can someone pass me one?" she asked. "I can't get it from here."

The games always started like this: The running scroll of a warning filed across the bottom of the screen. They'd given the show an advisory rating, warning people that there was a real chance of death.

Kyle sat down with Jerry and Chloe on the couch, on its fraying armrest. They had made a point to watch one episode together as a family a week, and tonight the flashing neon of the monitor read, *Do You Want To Live Your Best Life?* Sometimes, out the window, Kyle could see his neighbors settling in for a viewing, the shifting shadows of their bodies through the curtains. Recently, he'd tried not to look. Their movement through the windows made them look like contestants inside a television.

On the screen, the host summoned the family members in their glass boxes. There were three tonight: two brothers and a sister. Kyle couldn't imagine what had brought them to X, but it must have been something awful. In makeup, in close-up, they looked so young.

When all was settled, the sister began to cry. This happened occasionally. The cameras avoided her until she regained composure.

Jerry and Kyle hadn't spoken about whether to include

Chloe in these weekly viewings, but it was already decided that she'd likely find another way of seeing the show, and that this was a necessary part of preparation.

"First question," the host said. "What time does Erin like to eat dinner?"

The first brother offered his answer: seven. It was correct.

"I wonder if there's a way to quit," Chloe said.

"There isn't," Jerry said. Kyle gave him a look, and he shot one back. "I mean, not that I know of, but maybe."

There wasn't a way to quit. Kyle had considered this nightly as he fell asleep next to Jerry, the slight smear of purple makeup on his pillow—the residue of whatever show Jerry had done the night before. People outside X paid a lot to see the drag shows but tipped little. Jerry's job doing drag was actually a strong one, even for the little it brought in.

"I think they're going to win," Chloe said. "I just know it."

"You know," Kyle said, retying a small bow in her hair, "I think you're right."

"I'll look up how to quit," Chloe said. She sat up and combed her fingers through her hair.

The fact was, he knew, there *was* one way out now. The confetti fell like colorful snow inside a globe on the monitor, and Chloe clapped with relief. It was to win.

About a week before Kyle and his family were slated to appear on the show, there had been a riot downtown: buildings sprayed with the show's signature golden mist in wide

Xs and profane slurs: *Take your fucking $ and shove it* and *This is not human* and *We won't play much longer.* Kyle had to walk Chloe to school a long way to keep from seeing the mess, which still hadn't been cleaned up, even now.

These were the thoughts Kyle found himself orbiting, returning to again and again. There almost wasn't room for wanting anything at all but to be somewhere else. Maybe that was part of the game, he thought. Maybe that was the whole point.

He sat in his kitchen looking out the window, frost climbing slow on the glass from the radiator, snow falling outside. He couldn't sleep. The sun was beginning to rise, a thin line of warmth. He had been practicing the answers to possible questions, closed his eyes and considered them each:

Where would your father most like to travel? (Hawaii.)

What is your husband's greatest wish? (To win this show.)

Who does your father love more: his husband or you? (_____)

Kyle hated the last question the most. He didn't yet have an answer for it.

If there was an upside to *How to Live Your Best Life,* Kyle thought, it was that the show allowed for a few weeks of preparation, but this preparation was true code for torture. Sometimes Chloe would wake him up in the middle of the night, crying with a simple question she needed the answer to, something like, "Do you want to have another kid?" Or Jerry would turn on the pillow, eyes closed, and quietly ask, "Do you ever want me to stop doing drag?"

The last few weeks had been full of answers. He was telling Jerry and Chloe what he wanted, which was important because contestants had to answer two such questions consecutively and correctly, with three chances for error.

Kyle knew he should be asleep. He considered walking to the living room and rewatching an old episode, looking for clues, hints of repeated questions, common errors. The snow outside was almost imperceptible with the intensifying morning light. Jerry would be awake any moment, probably with another question, like, *What time would you wake up if you didn't have a job?* Something small, delivered with a slight sneer. The last few weeks had been full of answers, and Kyle didn't want most of them.

Kyle saw Jerry's shadow rise on the far wall and put the envelope back on the table. The radiator began to hiss, and he imagined its sound would wake Chloe, as it normally did.

"Any new wants?" Jerry asked him, per routine.

"I don't want to do this," Kyle said, standing up.

"You knew," Jerry said, "that's not how this works."

Jerry was fixing the braid in Chloe's hair when the black van pulled up in front of their apartment. It had been a long time since any of them had been in a car—weeks, Kyle knew, but how long exactly, he wasn't sure. Inside it, the air smelled like dust and smoke. The three buckled their seat belts.

"You look beautiful," Jerry told Chloe, adjusting the braid over her ear.

Kyle sat back in his seat, shifted his weight, and pulled on his shirt, which had begun to wrinkle. When he looked over, he saw Jerry, offering a look as if to say, *Here we go.* Kyle opened his palm to Chloe, and she took his hand. Then he opened his other hand to Jerry, closed his eyes, and waited. He felt warmth racing to his cheeks, and he nearly said, *Take my hand*, but kept himself from appearing too desperate. The car moved forward, their apartment shrinking in the rearview, the city growing on the horizon.

From backstage, the set seemed like a room made of light and sound. Kyle briefly saw it as he passed, the vacant seats like headstones before the stage. There were more than he'd imagined, a small stadium of them.

Feedback hit the stage.

"You'd think with all this money they could hire *professionals*," Jerry said, rolling his eyes.

Kyle wasn't sure why he had assumed they'd have a few minutes together, but just as soon as they had been escorted into the studio, its high ceilings and cement walls, two guards appeared. They led Jerry off to have his makeup done. "I can do it myself," he told them, fixing his hair in the dark glass of a sign that read, KEEP CALM. SMILE. YOU'RE ON NATIONAL TV.

"Dad!" Chloe called out after him.

Jerry turned his head and said, "Love you!" He strutted like he did on the bar runway. Kyle smiled at it and opened his mouth to say something but couldn't think of what, and by then Jerry had turned a corner and disappeared.

"Listen to me," Kyle said, turning back to Chloe. He knelt to her. "Do you know how many people have done this?"

"Hundreds," Chloe said without hesitation.

He didn't expect her to have the right answer, but then, he thought, when didn't she have the right answer?

"Right." He exhaled.

"Dad?"

"Yeah."

"I'm excited to live somewhere else."

He hugged her then—a slow, warm embrace. The heat of the show's lights lingered around them in a haze.

"And if they ask," Kyle said, "about which of you I'd save, if I had to only save one of you?"

He paused. He didn't know why he paused. He looked down, pinching the bridge of his nose. Was he performing the difficulty of the answer, or was it really this difficult? Two other guards arrived from behind him, one hand from each reaching for Chloe's shoulder.

"You," Kyle said. "I want you."

A man with a large headset handed Kyle a clipboard with the questions. He had a half hour to answer all of them. He made a point to keep his responses to one or two words. There were some that Jerry and Chloe would certainly get. And there were others he just didn't know. And a few summoned the image of that flashing X.

Kyle's face burned with the violent white spotlight, which he remembered seeing from the opening of so many episodes, the faces of contestants lit in a dangerous glow, their terror made obvious by the visibility of any scars, any sleeplessness from the night before. He couldn't see Jerry or Chloe, and his throat tensed with anticipation, the fever of nausea. What he tried to focus on was how he would forget this memory he was currently living inside, this moment with his trapped family set to arrive in their glass boxes, the distant movement of bodies shifting in their seats, the sick gleam of the host's teeth as he welcomed the audience to consider whether they wanted to live their best lives, and how.

Kyle noticed after everyone else, following energy directed upward, the little gasps of excitement: Jerry and Chloe inside of their boxes which hung in the air, held by glossy black chains. He almost swore. He'd seen the glass boxes in a variety of arrangements, stacked, placed on the ground, even dug beneath the stage. Once, their edges were licked by blue flames. Another time, on one of the anniversary episodes, the boxes sat within a great tank of water, which reddened with each incorrect answer in actual blood.

"So," the host said, turning to Kyle, his eyes drawn to Jerry and Chloe. "Do they know how you'd live your best life?"

The man turned away, his greasy hair catching the light like a mirror. Kyle looked up at Chloe, then at Jerry, who faced forward. Jerry was tapping his right heel nervously—

a habit Kyle had thought he'd grown out of years ago. It was hard to listen to the host, who spoke with thick enthusiasm, something Kyle knew better than to trust. Noise had faded, blurred into a static, almost, then turned to a piercing hum in his ears. It took Kyle a moment to recognize the noise as his microphone turning on.

"Let's find out," the man said, and then a great light appeared from behind Kyle—the game screen—making him look and feel like a shadow.

The red X appeared above Jerry. Time passed, rushing forward. Sound faded in and out, and at several moments Kyle felt delirious. There was that familiar sensation of getting away with something—but with what? He almost felt the wind racing past him as he tripped, routinely, running home with those things he'd stolen.

The red X flashed above Chloe without warning, and a weak trail of clear liquid began to file into her box. It pooled on the bottom in a translucent film. Kyle was relieved it wasn't blood, then wondered when the trail would stop, and what, exactly, it was. He heard a light thudding—Jerry pounding on his glass. It was against the rules. The show seemed to stop for a moment as the host received word from someone backstage. There was another question—one more before Chloe could lose, which she wouldn't.

And Kyle heard Jerry's dulled scream, like the fog of a whisper. *Let her go*, Kyle thought he was saying, but it was hard for anyone to tell for certain, and the show went to commercial as the water continued to flow slowly in.

The host unfolded the paper.

What crime would your father most want to commit?

The words seemed to sting the air. Kyle had answered, *Fraud*, something he'd joked with Jerry about—though how much of the joke Jerry understood, Kyle was unsure. He hadn't expected Chloe to receive the question when he'd written it—his pen shivering against the paper, the word spilling out of him like a secret—trying to remember what he'd told them he'd wanted, all those times.

The pause before Chloe's response was long, heavy with fear. Light saturated the stage, and that dust drifted in the air again. Kyle could hear people shifting in their seats. The host stretched the pause before Chloe was prompted to speak, and he wondered if they had cut to commercial. There was no great noise but a howling Kyle wished came from outside X, those sad dogs begging—but to what, and what for?

Her voice was small and polite, and it rang out amplified over the audience like a sentence.

"Robbery."

Kyle didn't believe he heard it at first. He was suddenly sure his life had dovetailed somewhere in the past months, frayed, that he'd slipped into a dream he felt vividly, awfully, and into the harsh light of his life. He hadn't sent that envelope; he hadn't signed on that line. He wasn't onstage. He couldn't be watching the scene on that great big screen behind him: Chloe turning like a trapped animal fifty feet in the air, water floating her white dress to her waist, the slight fogging inside, her hands pressed against the glass.

He looked up at his daughter, her blond hair shocked out in the bright water. The light came from behind and made her seem a silhouette. Like him, he thought. Monitors reflected off the dark glass of the set, showing her in close-up: cheeks inflated with air, face reddening slightly. Her eyes were closed in expectation of a correct answer. She was holding her breath as he'd taught her to. He wanted to run up to the glass and shatter it right there— water flooding the stage, shards glistening like confetti on the floor, a sudden, mortified gasp from the audience. He wanted to rewind the whole night, to sink into his old life. There had to be a way, he thought. People managed to erase all sorts of things every day: failures in marriages, in jobs. And just as he planned to turn to the main camera and punch it out, to shout, *Help me*, the buzzer sounded, and a thin golden mist was swiftly released into the tank.

Part II

YOU KNOW

PLEASE HOLD

The photo hangs crooked, like this—

I can barely hear Sal call, "Action!" over the wind, brown leaves turning up and scattering downhill. It is the final shot of the day, and standing in this mountain field—my back hit with the last rays of sun, red flannel shirt itching my arms—I think: Why was *I* cast as Andy? What about *my* online CastCall profile says, *Maybe a little out of his mind. Prefers being alone. Willing to risk his life for a snake.*

It is dusk, a line of gold light tipped over the Vermont mountains. We have to stop filming for *Lethal Instinct* every few minutes because Sal needs to "check the big game." The snake, which rests on a bed of dead oak leaves, from a certain angle—in silhouette, I'm told—*looks* real. Everything from the crew, who fight over a fast-food dinner, to the cameraman's broken chair suggests what I told myself I'd never do again: low budget. But this afternoon, and tonight, I'm Andy Campbell, a man bitten by one of the exotic snakes he kept as a pet before meeting his untimely death in the Catskills, having inappropriately projected human emotion onto a wild-caught king cobra. I am Andy Campbell, and my eyes are glazing evocatively over with tears. My legs are the first to go paralyzed, then my hands, and I fall to my knees to avoid facing the lens. I am Andy Campbell, alone in my field. I was cast out by society for my love of reptiles and made my home in a cabin flanked by old pines. I own several forgotten vials of antivenom, and I don't have time to call my brother before the pain seizes my arms, fills them with dead weight. I'm not clear on what motivates me to handle the snake improperly, and Sal says he can't tell me. "No one really knows," he says. I am a dead mystery, and I did not have a history of bad decisions. I twitch just once before dying.

"We're gonna run three takes, just in a row," Sal yells.

"Sure," I say. It sounds just how I want it to—so *over it, done before*. I've been trying to project confidence. Four years ago when I started doing these films, I thought it was a way out of something, and now I realize it's only a way in—to doing more of these films, which could more aptly be called "stints," a term my mother has taken to using in place of my preferred "jobs."

"Action!" Sal yells.

I walk a few steps down the hill, kneel to the snake, upstaging it so the camera can't see. I try to move with the kind of nonchalant gait I'd expect from someone like Andy, a sort of *whatever* in every movement. I pause for a few beats, preparing for the imagined bite. When it strikes,

I bring my thumb to my teeth and snip the skin hard—snap back my arm, shake my hand, and bring the bite wound to my lips, a small circle of dark red pooling near the base of my thumb. Andy Campbell would have learned to suck out the venom.

After that pause, I walk back up, trying to forget the actual sting of the bite. I regret having broken the skin. In the wind, my blood feels cool. It's almost evening, the time Andy actually died, but Sal calls out to say I've done a good take, and that they don't need any more. The crew briefly cheers, announcing that the filming for the series is over. This was it.

But as I shake the stinging numbness from my thumb, I consider that none of this is *technically* the problem. The problem, technically, I can't forget. Even as I let my neck grow slack, that thin orange glow on the horizon in my peripheral vision and the small lens shooting my smaller reflection back at me in the sudden cold, I think about it. My boyfriend Cole is lying on an operating table struck with sterile white light, and a man with a green mask over his nose and mouth is holding out his hand and saying, "Scalpel."

I *did* know what moving in with Cole would look like. Sort of.

And Cole had always been defensive about his work, something I felt I couldn't, as another aspiring artist, ever invalidate. So I didn't press the point. But I did not know, not at all when I opened the screen door with that faded duffel at my side, backpack a lead weight on my shoulders, not at all before climbing those wood steps to the porch, what his life looked like—really. After three years spending nights in each other's dorm room, it was all perfect—or as close to perfect as I could see the word: him with his paint-splattered overalls, his wide-lens camera and rolls of tan film, and me with my scripts, the rehearsals and auditions, replaying single scenes for hours. That was the expectation.

So when he saw me trying to get the door that day, fumbling with the strap on my bag, he turned the handle. I bumped awkwardly in. He kissed me—that unchanged tongue-first kiss. I hit my head against the low doorframe as he pushed me and we both fell down. The tile floor was hot with sunlight as we smiled into each other. And then there he was on top of me when I saw the first warning sign.

It was not hard to discern, at the time, what it was hanging on the wall, or why I didn't ask about it. The photograph. But I didn't get a good look at it. In fact, at first, I wondered if I saw it at all.

But that didn't matter to me then. Because in an instant I was back again—to those years before I knew what it felt like to be adrift in the world, to intimately know the phrase "cattle call," before those few months when I didn't have Cole, trying to make it alone, so I could run back to him with proof of my worth. *See!* I wanted to say, months later. Before the backup plan was to move to New York, take up with some small theater, and hope for someone to stop me, to beg me into a job. And that place was so warm, so what

I wanted, even the room disappeared around us. He pushed off my backpack, and I closed my eyes. I felt ridiculous to be that romantic. The tile lifted beneath me like a cloud.

The hill seems steeper, at least the way I'm going down, stopping every few moments to pause at the reflective eyes of chipmunks. The dark settles in like a gray mist around me. I'm surprised I'm not being walked down by the crew, who decided to stay put to get some cold open footage of the sunset. *Lethal Instinct*. I can almost see it already flash, tacky, across a screen.

My phone rings—I didn't think I had service. I lose my footing on a slick boulder trying to fish it out of a loose pocket. For some reason, I thought Andy Campbell would wear baggy clothes, clothes he could drown in—my own misprojection. As it turns out, Sal showed me a photo of Andy—young Andy, back when he was social and full of promise, and he was handsome, something the description of him hadn't mentioned and something I hadn't actually considered a possibility—wearing a denim jacket, his brown hair parted and slicked back. Sal let me wear what I had brought, and it felt like a betrayal of character, but I didn't want to argue the point and risk seeming high maintenance.

"Hey, buddy." I have to pause to hear Sal. "We were talking, me and the crew, we were talking," he says. I detect he needs something more from me. A drop of rain hits my nose, and I look up, move nearer to the trunk of a tree. "We were wondering if you wanna shoot that scene again.

Right now, soon as you can. Joey looked over it and it just looks, well, you know."

I can hear rain falling over trees. I consider what I did wrong. People tell you it's the light or some bullshit about angles. No. If you have to redo a take, you did something wrong.

"It's something about the light," Sal says.

"It is pretty dark out," I say, sure he's seeing the same night I am. My mind runs back to the question: How I had messed up. I went through Andy's thinking as best I could beforehand, scribbled in black ink in my notebook back at Cole's: *If I were Andy,* I wrote, *I'd have gone searching for that snake. I'd have overturned every leaf, looked behind every rock, and just when I thought it futile, called off my search, there it would be: coiling like a garden hose in dense weeds.* I'd see it and then the snake would get me. Like that. No explanation. The notes weren't helpful, but suggested I was serious about my roles, so I had cultivated the habit early in my career.

But then I realize: Was Andy being impatient? Maybe *that's* it. That's the reason he couldn't save that snake from the Vermont forest, the winter, when it would surely die. Maybe he was so happy he finally found it, he couldn't think clearly. It was, after all, the moment of rescue. And what else did Andy have?

I tell Sal I'm walking back up, to expect me. With every step, I consider that acting would be a gift, if I could do it either much better or much worse. If someone had told me in middle school, as I acted out *Macbeth* to an audience of ten, that I wasn't cut out for this, gotten me on another path, an office job that would have let me take care of myself. Or if I could have signed with an agent during school, fast-tracked past the shit gigs. Just before I see the outline of the dark clearing ahead, a calm wind slanting its tall grass, I notice a voicemail, delivered to my phone sometime these past few minutes when I wasn't paying attention. The voice is low, and I have to pause again to make it out. I catch—"this does not look good. Please give us a call back when you can. I'm sorry to concern you, but this is truly urgent."

The word "truly" feels hard and wrong, too formal.

"Hey!" Sal spots me from the field. He's waving both his arms, like that's the only way I'll notice him, like I don't get subtlety. I raise a hand as if to say, *Wait a minute*, as if I'm on the phone with someone, but then there is the sharp beep against my ear and I am frozen in place. I move my foot forward but I feel sick. I am sick. I am on the ground, and my eyes are watering, my palms against the fallen wet leaves, a sick metal taste behind my molars. "You ready?" he yells down to me. My lungs seize. The air is so clean it hurts to breathe. The inky night pitches in and out of focus, and I feel a drop of rain strike the back of my neck, faster. "Just one more," he adds. And then, louder, "We promise!"

Cole lived in an enormous cabin in the middle of New Hampshire. It was beautiful, a sort of vacation home, wrapped in porch, with more window than wall. It seemed to have been designed around how much sunlight would enter, and from which angles, and at what times. When I woke up the next morning, and Cole was still asleep, it felt as if I had been startled awake. It was the hard light shooting in through his blinds—more expensive blinds, I noticed, than I had expected. And the red sheets were so soft. I made a note to ask about thread count over breakfast, whenever he woke.

But a half hour later—like in college, when I came back from the dining hall to find him still asleep in my bed—he wasn't awake. I stayed near him, watched him turn over, but even at noon he was asleep. I got up and took a shower, only using his soap; the shampoo was foreign and looked expensive. Cole always had this sort of taste, ever since I met him in Introduction to Acting: no dining hall food, packages of imported things from his parents, a cultivated fondness for something that looked like caviar but was in fact both rarer and more expensive. After the shower, I dressed and, noticing Cole still asleep, walked to the kitchen.

And there it was.

It was not a photo of just any man, but a beautiful man—blond with those darker highlights, those chiseled abs I could never get no matter how I starved myself, the sort of brooding face that suggested real thought. The worst part: Cole's florid signature beneath it, like he had some claim to the man. The photo hung above Cole's kitchen sink, and I immediately imagined him seeing it, enjoying it, every day, every time he saw it. I looked closer, and the whole thing came into sharp, revolting relief.

None of this would have been a problem, I reminded myself, my stomach burning with anxiety—not if it hadn't been for the day senior year I walked in on Cole while I skipped a lecture on Lessac theory, my copy of his key turning in that lock, and those loud and hurried whispers, and the black sheets over his pale chest. I had heard Cole once discussing a photo he had taken of this same man as his best to date. "Not because he's attractive," Cole had said, but because the man had been on the verge of tears after his own breakup, which made for *excellent photography*, "real emotion." The wind struck me as I walked back to my room, shaking. None of this would have been a problem. The photo would not have been a problem.

I heard footsteps and turned around. "Morning," Cole said, rubbing his eye with a palm. I pointed at the photograph without looking at it again, that stupid body backlit with white light. I mustered in a quick rage some of the best acting advice I had ever received, years before during an audition: If you want to sound serious, speak a question as if it's a fact.

"Oh," he said, blinking the sleep out of his eyes.

Outside, a cicada held its shriek.

"What is this," I said.

"You look awful."

This, of course, is Sal, who has everything set up for another shot. But he's taken the light away. The problem, he says, was it looked artificial. It looked made. I wanted to steal away, only for a minute, to call the doctor and learn what was happening with Cole, what they'd found. The red rash that had spread suddenly like a map across his back days ago, the blood that had come to the corner of his lip in a clot after breakfast. A fang through us both.

But Sal had asked, "Can it wait?" And I had said yes— something that, unlike projecting confidence, I'm trying *not* to do. To say yes to everything. I hold my thumb and make a point not to bite it again. I can feel it still, the glow and pulse of pain.

So everything gets reset. Sal stops telling the crew to "find the wind" and to move the snake just so. I have no lines. I just redo the part where I die.

But after Sal calls, "Action!" something clicks on like a lamp, and I start walking with a different step. It feels almost as if I'm possessed, like my body knows all the right things to do. My eyes are mad with fear. I make a false pass at a log, looking for the snake, which I've suddenly given a name—Emily—that name is just spinning in my mind, and I've lost her, why had I left the lid of her tank open last night, and where could she be, really, and then I see her. And I move my hand down, something I've never had to do before—her tank is on the top shelf, above the scorpions— and I don't have time to kneel. I feel how Andy does: as if the world has dealt me an unfair hand, I think, but not in the way people reference it—like even the cards themselves are meant for another game. I'm on the ground, my forehead slick with sweat, but before I can keep on with the scene, Sal has jumped off his chair. "Holy shit!" he says.

Behind him, one of the crew members tosses up his hands and says, "Sal, come on. You just fucked up the shot."

My shirt is weighed down in the humidity, the flannel choice seeming smarter every minute, my personal spin on a role so unlike me. I'm overcome by a sense of pride, the feeling I've reached some new height, adrenaline tripping my heartbeat.

"Turn on the lights!" Sal says. He hops back on his chair, pleased with himself. "For fuck's sake. Give him some light. That was"—he pauses, unaccustomed to thinking before speaking—"excellent."

There is a cut-open quality to the moment, a vulnerability that feels violent. I sit up and brush the burrs from my knees. Above, the moon glows yellow, but it instantly disappears when a flash of stark, hot light floods my vision. I can see the rain fall, barely, through the harsh glow. I cover my eyes with my hand, the scabbed red dot on my thumb uglier than I expected. From this angle it actually looks like a snakebite. The crew flicks on another light behind me.

"Now that?" Sal adds. "*That* was acting."

It didn't take long to rehash the basics: Cole had been doing this since senior year, when he'd photograph models in an unused room in the Engineering building, which was never locked and near his studio, since he realized how well it paid; he was still trying to sell his nature photographs to major magazines; he preferred other art; this was temporary, probably; he loved me—he really did—so, what was the problem?

"The problem," I said, "is, like, five problems."

"Start with one." Cole had the awful habit of getting me

to talk by making the discussion seem doable, the problems solvable, even easy.

"Where do you even *do* this now?"

"Here," he said, and tried to take my hand. "I'll show
you."

He brought me to the top of the cellar staircase, his
hand shaking. I wondered how he thought I'd react once I
did find out he was still doing this, because I was *going* to
find out—he had the photo above his sink, for God's sake,
and then it occurred to me maybe this was a sign of how
desperate he perceived me to be, that he knew I would love
him despite it.

"Shit," he said. He held the silver door handle and
looked at me, his eyes shot with red. The sunlight grew
across the living room, reached us and faded. "You're going to freak out."

Another one of Cole's habits: He tended to be right.

The view of basement registered in the same way as a
scene I once played in college for an original horror-drama
entitled *Please Hold*. All of my lines (and the play itself)
were bad. I had taken the part, given out of some ridiculous pity from a professor who considered me a depart-
ment underdog, which was embarrassing. In the film, I
was a secretary entering middle age, and every other scene
had me answering the phone at my work, several times,
and saying those words: "Please hold." In the final scene,
though, I realized my daughter had left her bedroom after
curfew, taken off with a handsome, volatile football player
with a drug problem and a collection of samurai swords on

his bedroom wall. "You have to seriously imagine the trouble," the director said. His words held weight, and I imagine he could feel them reflected in his own life.

And so I did. I imagined, seriously, the scene's "emotional turning," a phrase used to describe the advancing of emotion through a split-second moment. It was one of our college's *things*, a proud central lesson of the curriculum. The idea was there are moments inside of moments that we can never know but have to try to replicate. My emotional turning for the scene, my hand on my head, jaw gone slack, eyes scanning that room, registered like this: 1. Fear for my daughter → 2. Anger at her having broken her promise to me → 3. Concern over how I would be perceived by those close to me → 4. Disbelief that it had ever happened, that I had ever lost her, at all → 5. The lockdown of definite loss.

So when I saw the photos, gold framed and winking on the wall, I was furious. I turned to Cole, expecting my body to will forward a punch. But when I saw the bed in the center of the room, made cleanly with those same red sheets I had slept in the night before, I collapsed into disbelief. I sighed and sat down on the cold cement stairs.

"Cole," I said.

"I can explain," he said.

"Haven't you already." I felt myself press the period into that sentence.

At the end of that play, I returned to that bedroom, and my daughter was still gone, and that was when the lights for the act went down. Cole was in the audience, watching me, though I couldn't see him. He later told me I had looked directly at him, but I don't remember that. And before the hot light shut down, it grew intensely, furiously bright, so that when I was left standing near her bookcase, my hand on the small of my back, I appeared as a ghost in the sudden dark.

It is night now. I run through the scene again, one last time, and my heart is wild, like I released something I didn't know was in me to begin with, something that kept the other parts of me lodged in their correct places. I'm on the ground, again, my hair coated with dew, the rain shower now a pervasive mist, like I'm filming in a dream. We just finished three more takes of the same scene, with variations on where I first thought I'd seen the snake: under a log, near my foot, and once—"So exciting!" Sal had said—behind the lens, from the snake's point of view.

A flock of small birds trembles up from tall trees, like thrown ash across the deep blue sky. I wait for Sal to finish talking to his assistant, a sad man wearing an awful old earpiece whose main job is to strike the time code clapper.

"So we were thinking," Sal says again. He walks toward me, a silhouette. "We were just talking and, wow—something changed in you." He stops just short of stepping into where he'd be in the shot, halfway illuminated. I can see his squinted eyes, sense good news.

"How'd you like to do one more scene?" he says. "Just, you know, to try it?"

I had nearly forgotten what had caused my change, so wrapped up in *how* I'd changed, how I was being recognized for my ability and not my crooked nose or whatever I'd written on my CastCall profile (*Leading man or supporting man: I do both!*)—the headshot Cole had taken and generously edited: How many jobs had that got me?—that had attracted Sal in the first place. I need to call the doctor back. I'm vaguely disgusted I haven't yet. In fact, I *feel* disgusting, covered in dirt, my shirtsleeve awkwardly rolled up, the rain giving me an undone, feral look.

"Can I have a minute?" I ask him.

"It'll only *take* a minute," he says.

"What's the scene?" I say.

He turns around and gives his assistant the thumbs-up; the man runs to turn off several lights moths had started to buzz around. He shuts off all but one, as if I already agreed to doing the take. A current of wild air rattles and knocks over a folding chair. It's freezing, I realize, and the hair on my arm shivers up, my blood cold as a cobra's, and I'm reminded of Cole, and how pale he was three weeks ago.

"Oh, it's the same part," Sal says. "Where you die. Sort of." He pauses as he settles back into his chair and whispers something to his assistant. "We just want it zoomed in. We want it slowed down. Think you can do that for us?"

The way Cole and I decided to get over it—after I briefly cried out on the porch, a thunderstorm coming, and went back inside, after we ordered dinner and he told me between bites of pasta curled around his fork that *he loved me*, he was doing this *for us*—was to not talk about it, and to create a code for when a client was coming in. When he said, "Looks like bad weather," I'd know. He was sensitive to my idiot grief, and I both admired and hated him for it, because that meant nothing would change. I finally unpacked my things in his dresser that night, convinced I could *do* this, that I could stay.

That night, after Cole fell asleep, I stayed awake thinking about emotional turning. The window was open; the air smelled like moss. It wasn't just Cole. I had been so blindly trusting in my acting coaches. Once, years ago as a rehearsal warm-up exercise, the cast was asked to become ice cream cones on "a hot July boardwalk" (*weirdly specific*, I recalled thinking), and I melted stupidly to the floor. Why had I done this? Why hadn't I asked more questions? Had I grown from this moment? Softened further? And then the question I dreaded: Why did I act at all? I was soft serve vanilla melting from that moment, melting still.

Closing my eyes, I found instead of rest the image of Cole's photo, hanging in the kitchen. Looking at me. The model reached one hand out of the glossy film and onto the wall; his other hand steadied itself on the photo base, and he lifted himself out—right there onto the tile floor, nude. His muscular shadow stood in the bedroom doorframe, watching Cole and me under the covers. I wondered if this would stir anything in Cole, and what that would be.

Before I fell asleep, I was thrown back into that scene in *Please Hold*: The director pleaded to me, red faced, looking at the notes from our last dress rehearsal. "What have you *won*?" He seemed drunk at the time, and spat a bit with passion. It occurred to me I didn't understand the question but that my admission of this would only rouse in him a storm. I said, "Nothing."

"That's right," I remember him saying, pleased with himself and me. "*Nothing.*"

Sal gave me only a minute to figure out my emotional turning. I decided Andy Campbell's final moment would go something like this: 1. Shock at having mishandled the snake → 2. Shock that the snake I loved, that I had cared for, bit me → 3. A strong surge of purple venom through my neck, seizing all other thought → 4. The knowledge I will die → 5. Both the lightness of fainting and that final sting of regret for ever having moved out to the mountains, for losing all the people of my life, for becoming so completely resigned to begin with.

We run the take, though I don't move in it. I close my eyes and pace through the emotions as if they are a flipbook, touching each and just as swiftly moving to the next, wincing, letting every minute difference appear barely, even risking its loss on the viewer. Only for a second I consider whether I am trying out any of what Cole is feeling right now, those yellow plastic bands around his arm, a clear IV stuck in his elbow, his head shaved and reflective, almost greasy. Here, filming as Andy Campbell, the Vermont mountains like dark teeth jutting up around me, I wonder if I have already lost him.

"I don't know what you're doing these little jobs for," Sal says. "Tell you what, I'll be in touch." He moves forward to shake my hand but sees my thumb.

"How'd that happen?" he asks.

"I fell coming up." I try to make it sound convincing, and it does. "Wet leaves."

"So that's why you looked awful." He laughs. It offends me and then it doesn't. There is a distant clap of thunder. Wind races through the trees, trembling the leaves.

"Huh," Sal's assistant says. It's the first I've heard his voice, which is mousy and thin, not at all what I had expected. He removes his earpiece and holds a palm up in the air. The lights click off behind him, and my eyesight doesn't adjust right away. The man says, "Better head out. Looks like some pretty bad weather."

"It's called *Lethal Instinct*," I yelled. It was a warm night, almost a month after I had arrived at Cole's place. He was downstairs, uploading photos onto the computer. He'd stopped doing the prints at my urging; the profit was better online anyway, and most of his models didn't mind— better exposure. Not that I ever saw them. I always made a point to hide away or drive to town whenever he had the men over. I avoided my occasional desire to go downstairs, to uncover anything, because I had nowhere else to go.

"This guy," I said, scrolling down, reading the description of Andy Campbell. "This guy had over fifty snakes, Cole! In a *trailer*."

"He did what?" Cole asked. His voice was deadened from the other room.

I briefly considered this, what Andy had done, but I was trying to get down to my point: a freak. This guy must have been a freak to do something like this—however he'd even managed it. Hauling tanks and snakes up a mountain, something I couldn't even picture. And what kind of guy, the thought distracted, got cast in that role anyway? How does *that* mind work?

Through the kitchen window I saw a flock of crows settle on the branches of a tree. I sat down at the table again and squinted at Andy's physical specs, the actor's desired height and weight and features. It was me right there on the screen, down to the note about a particular kind of nose.

The sun dimmed quickly, like a lamp clicked off, and I felt myself stiffen in my chair as I read on, looking up occasionally to see the birds, to wonder about where they'd come from and why they hadn't moved. When I went downstairs to check on Cole, he got the story wrong: He thought I'd said Andy bit the snake. He looked as he had when I'd first seen him, a blue button-down, attentive eyes, that messy brown hair styled in a perfect swoop, all that energy of love coming at me like a breeze from across the quad, too easy to be anything real. And I could see his computer screen in the reflection of a glass cabinet behind him: some man like me, maybe, or not—I could only make out the frame, and it occurred to me for the first time that if it were me, with my eye behind the lens, I would not know how I would pose Cole, which angles might flatter, what it would mean to say, *Stand like this, I want to see you like this.*

Lethal Instinct comes out two weeks after Cole closes his eyes for the last time. He leaves me with the whole house and his business, and each night I look up how to shut it all down, but I haven't brought myself to do anything yet. I don't touch the photos. With Cole's gorgeous signature in each, they've taken on a haunted quality, and I am superstitious of everything. The messages just add up in his inbox: *Still on for next week?* There is evidence of nothing I had felt, all those suspicions I had hissing away in my mind. A model showed up a few days ago at the door, his blond hair cut for the occasion, and I just stared at him, feeling a fury grow in me, before saying Cole wasn't around. A euphemism that felt sinful.

And when I'm being honest? I know what's true. I know that I had given myself my own snakebite when, days after seeing Cole in bed with that model, after we'd decided to just get over it, I met a guy at a dive bar and went—proudly, decisively—home with him. A secret sealed so deep within me it began to fester and spread. I had all the upper hand I could ask for, but I still wonder if all the emotion I keep down is why I can't act for anyone other than myself. Every time I get upset, I take it over the top, because there's twice as much as I let myself feel. One bite either kills you or gives you fangs. I look down at my thumb. No evidence, so how will I know it had ever been me?

The show is somehow even less of a feature than I'd imagined, remade to a short docuseries on exotic animals that kill their fawning owners. I turn up the volume and sit on the couch, a pillow Cole had bought on my chest. The house had been so much his creation that the pain of his absence feels often, in the past days, like something I invent myself.

Watching this is a form of masochism, I know, but this particular way of hurting feels also like a way of honoring Cole, a logic that I know doesn't add up. My body tenses during the opening credits. Someone on the crew must have learned more about Andy, because the narrator starts confidently with facts about his childhood, stock footage of babies an embarrassing precursor to my scene with the snake. Andy's mom had died of cancer when he was young. He loved snakes especially, though he also kept a pair of pigeons and tried to train them to carry messages— something a neighbor awkwardly divulged in anonymous silhouette during a cut scene. I find it unbelievable that there is a neighbor in Andy's story at all, the man who found him slumped there against his trailer a few days later, a poisonous cobalt hue marbling Andy's hand and wrist. That Andy had given up on people seemed to be the general point of his adolescence, and though I was waiting with some excitement for information that would surprise me, the obviousness of this felt right.

I don't see at first that the crew had decided not to use me at all. They had gone with a different actor, someone who didn't even type the part: a thick head of wild brown hair, muscular arms. Played up the handsome. They gave him another story, took liberties. I only see that it was another Andy at that shot from the snake's point of view—so stupid, but I feel it in me, a betrayal that can be any size I want, another little pulse of venom in my veins that I know I'll survive. When the credits roll, I don't bother looking for my name. I stand and walk to the kitchen. The light from a candle catches on each mounted photo, that glass hiding those wild secrets I had put there myself, those little monsters, my reflection in every frame.

BE ALIVE

We're on our way to the city, finally, when Glen tells me that the chainsaw got him this time. He was out of ammo and extra lives, so he hid under the bed. "Who knew," he says, looking out the car window at the bright night skyline, "zombies could crawl?"

Early December. The roads are still without ice, but the air is bit through with cold. My boyfriend Glen and I are driving to a dinner with his parents in Chicago, a city I loathe for its constant bleakness, the way you can turn a street corner and be jarred into another gray atmosphere. Glen once used the phrase "melting pot" to describe the city, the place he's from—a reminder he's seventeen years younger than me and still not clear that almost everywhere is a melting pot. Some places just wear the title better than others.

"Which is crazy, right?" Glen says. "*Thinking* zombies. With chainsaws."

"That is crazy," I say. "Aren't zombies not conscious?" I try my best to make it sound rhetorical, to erase the top of the question mark. I can hear myself using lawyer-voice, sounding leave-me-alone bored, like I do at work.

"Exactly," he says. "It's crazy. Be dead or be alive—I mean, come on."

This is what upsets you? I almost say. But I sense the awkward shine it would give the conversation. So I say nothing.

Here is what I'm not saying: Three hours ago, I learned that my brother has been committed, finally, to the psych wing of Mass General for swallowing the bleach our mother keeps hidden behind the washer. It is like the universe is saying, *Deal with this. Look at this. Acknowledge this.* Which is to say, I no longer care that Glen's parents will learn I am not, in fact, twenty-six. Or that I am likely to pay for another dinner I cannot comfortably afford. This is to say my brother has now absolutely missed the part where he transitions to being self-sufficient. My mother's words through the phone: *Mark, he is never going to get there.*

"I shouldn't have lied," I say. I rest a hand on Glen's knee. "About my age."

"You look thirty," he says. And then, more sincerely, "Really."

This is another problem: I'm in love with Glen, a love misunderstood by even many of my gay friends. Sometimes I think it hurts too much, to feel in my blood the interrogating thought of others when I'm around him. And then I imagine my life without him.

I slow for our exit, signal the turn. There is a chain of cars ahead of us, their lights blinking red. Glen starts again about a zombie that came after him with a syringe. He was running up these cement stairs, so many stairs, and the zombie was gaining on him. But it was a new release of the game. They let it out too soon, he says, with this glitch— those stairs didn't end. He just kept running, but it didn't matter how far, and then there was the blood dripping down the screen, and there was the refund, and how unrealistic is that anyway, a zombie that can think like that, that knows what it wants and always gets it.

BREATHING UNDERWATER

Gavin had told Jay he was a professional diver on their second date, almost four years ago, and had avoided all water-related activities since. The lie wouldn't have been a problem if Jay's cousin wasn't, as luck would have it, an Olympic hopeful swimmer. Or if Jay hadn't always—as he put it—loved the way a man's body "rose and dove in a single motion" through a current, which was his response when Gavin told him, across that restaurant table, that he spent his early twenties glistening like a mirage in radiant blue water, his body hit with those shining fluorescent lights as he shot past the black lines in record speed. Ever since, Gavin didn't have to actually defend the lie to Jay so much as either pretend to be sick, or injured, whenever swimming was called for, which wasn't often. He got cramps when Jay wanted to go to the pool. He developed a convincing and unexpected allergy to chlorine.

The problem started the day Gavin and Jay had taken their Sunday picnic from the town green to the lip of Black Lake, a body of water twenty miles inland of Cape Cod's coast that was known for looking like a pupil from the sky. It was early summer, the grass hot and dead under the cloth. Jay moved closer to Gavin and rested his hand on his thigh, biting into an apple, just as Gavin noticed the small head a dozen yards into the brown water, the tiny hand slapping noiselessly. So unlike him, Gavin had forgotten his lie just then. When he stood, his knee struck Jay's brow, and Gavin sensed him wince and turn away as he dove into that boiling brown water, the pebbled bottom digging into his chin. He swam out fast and saw—a child, the body submerged, air bubbles pocking the surface of the water. What he remembered next was the cold metal of the small white lifeboat that had appeared, rocking with the lurch of CPR, and the sight of families standing onshore, and Jay, holding his eye with ice wrapped in a checkered cloth napkin, smiling like an idiot.

Jay, vision clouded with tears, missed seeing Gavin out there in the water, and a father on the beach approached Jay—a reporter for the local news. Jay spilled every detail about Gavin, his "partner"—a word Jay had avoided using to describe them until then. But this was that one problem, coming up for air from the depths: Jay had unloaded all those years of who Gavin was. Including, of course, how good Gavin was with kids, his sixth sense for when food was about to burn, how long they had been together, and his status as once a record-holding swimmer, best in state.

Gavin held a golden memory of his first important lie. He remembered how the words had tumbled out in a way he almost couldn't control, how easy—even clean—it was to tell Erin before gym class that he could see the future, that he'd seen it before. He had said this as a fun distraction he'd decided split second. When prompted for a prophecy, Gavin shut his eyes, listening to the sound of basketballs hitting the shining linoleum floor. He concentrated on his breathing and told her she would be famous one day.

"How?" she asked, skeptical.

"I think it's singing," Gavin had said. "Or dancing. Something. When you get nervous you sing to yourself."

Gavin had heard from a classmate that Erin had taken to humming annoyingly to herself during quizzes in English. He took the easy leap of imagining she enjoyed it, that he could flatter her into believing.

Erin looked a little stunned, pleasantly surprised, and Gavin felt the same about what he'd just done. What he didn't realize, before stepping off the bleachers and standing against the padded wall to be picked for softball, was that Erin would tell her friends, and they would tell their friends. The next day during homeroom, several others came asking. Gavin had good visions for them, too, took what he knew of them and, like recombinant DNA, or even magic, made whole a future in which every suspicion of success was prophecy. Those seeds he planted, surrounding him and growing, like invasive weeds. Walls trapping him in a room, alone.

Gavin woke to the sound of the television crackling with static. It had been a long night of talking—mostly about the dumb pride Jay now felt about Gavin—and it occurred to Gavin often since only one day of pulling that child up and out of the water that he should feel proud too; or, if not proud, exactly, *something* good. He should feel he had saved something, because he had, after all. But it registered differently for Gavin, as if he'd only let something slip, like he had sealed his fate as someone who would inevitably be exposed for who he truly was.

"Guess who made the news?" Jay said, sitting down at the foot of the bed.

Gavin leaned over Jay's shoulder, resting his head on the hard bone, a move that felt pathetic though he intended it to seem romantic. There was a short, looping clip of the boy, Brady, that must have been shot after Gavin and Jay had left, because he was smiling, shivering in his pink towel. The reporter announced the boy's status as all right despite the close call. Gavin felt those words shoot back at him, as if it was really *his* close call, and was quietly pleased he had accidentally struck Jay, kept him from seeing anything.

Gavin hoped there was no footage of the rescue at risk of surfacing. At any moment, he feared he'd see it. He had the embarrassed words "Oh God" ready to force out, were the broadcast to zoom in on him thrashing out there on the water like a child. The superhero quality they'd given Gavin would be ruined by the sight of him diving idiotically into what was essentially a shallow swamp. That Jay had so adamantly claimed Gavin as his "partner" on that small beach, a moment Gavin remembered in vivid color, and was not identified as such in the segment, came off to Gavin as at best passively homophobic.

"They don't say you're my partner," Gavin said, lying back down. The pillow gave a deflating sigh as he rested his head on it.

"I didn't even notice," Jay said, which was the wrong response. And then, after a pause, thank God—"Maybe they thought it was obvious."

Gavin considered who might call him on the lie as he tried to fall back asleep. It was inevitable, he thought—someone would. The most sport he played in his early twenties was a brief stint as a beginning tap dancer, a hobby he gave up after not being the immediate best in a room full of aspiring dancers at his university. The benefit to moving far away from his home and life in Iowa to follow Jay to Massachusetts was that Gavin knew no one, which he found refreshing and freeing. But this, he began to consider, was its own illusion. Through the entire broadcast, he could see his reflection like a vision on the glass, there only when he focused on it.

After a while, a few of the things Gavin had said began to reveal themselves as true. Chad in the eighth grade made early junior varsity soccer at the high school, and Anna *did* get the lead in the school musical. It didn't matter that these things were expected, a notion that dawned on Gavin often, or that just as many of his peers had nothing come to fruition. The air around him began to feel vaguely dangerous, the ground beneath him slippery.

He held a kind of power, he thought, but it was false. But then, he sometimes wondered—was it?

––––––––––

The boat outing was meant to be a celebration, a thank-you, held by Brady's parents. The two had come over several nights after the rescue—that was what they'd called it, "rescue"—and offered Gavin, among other things, money. Lou and Louise, a stockbroker and an art teacher at a private high school, bled apology and gratitude in a way that unsettled Gavin. Then as they all sat down to a dinner of homemade pasta, Lou and Louise explained the boat party—all the details were planned, and that it was meant to be a surprise for him but Jay hadn't been sure when Gavin would have to be at work again—so they came out with it now. Gavin felt briefly locked in to something, then soothed himself with the reminder he would not have to swim. The boat party was a kind, benign gesture. He thanked them and said *they* were looking forward to it, that lone word a nod toward their now-labeled partnership.

"We weren't even sure where he'd gone," Lou said after a while, slapping a spoonful of sauce on his plate. "If it weren't for you—" His eyes met Louise's. Did they care about each other this much—was this ultraromantic eye contact real? Gavin wondered. Lou had said these words, or words like them (If it weren't for you! *How cartoonish.*), dozens of times in the, what, twenty minutes the four had been eating, and Gavin could sense it affecting him. Why couldn't everyone just *move on*? he thought before remembering he'd saved a child's life. He wanted to pawn off what he'd done, though, pass it like a bowl to the person next to him. To refuse the credit. If it weren't for him, he told himself, Brady would have been fine. He could almost see the child splashing up, unharmed, near the long reeds. Perfectly unharmed.

There was a pause as Jay poured wine, an expensive bottle Louise had handed him when they walked in. In the past, Gavin had been wary of Jay's drinking. It was true that Jay once had a "drinking problem," which was how Jay described it, something he had told Gavin after several dates. Gavin had never seen anything concerning, no behavior to suggest the problem, though he often found himself looking for vestiges, proof of it. He appreciated that Jay was forthcoming even as he envied the ability to be so open. Loathed it, actually.

Louise moved her napkin to her lap. "How far down did you dive?"

"It wasn't that far," Gavin said.

"He told me Brady was a ways down," Jay said, coiling the pasta around his fork. "I thought you said that?"

"It was kind of far, hard to remember," Gavin said. He felt the authority of fact slipping away from him and added, "Maybe a few yards."

But he remembered as he took a sip of the wine, nodding across the table at Lou, who held his wife's hand tenderly, that it was barely a couple of feet. He could see himself transported—back inside that screen—to that exact moment, his breathing labored, the tickle of stirred-up weeds on his neck, warmth rushing to his chin, where a few drops of blood had collected from scraping the bottom of the lake, and that shock of blond hair waving gently under the almost alien algae-green water, sinking into darkness.

Secure from his small fortunes coming to light in his class-mates, Gavin figured out that he could choose to see far into the future without repercussion. Amy would get into a top college for acting; Brad would drop out of high school but for something much better—Gavin couldn't see what yet, something to do with cars? Pit crew, NASCAR? (He had seen a racing magazine in Brad's backpack days before when he'd opened it to retrieve homework during class.) Gavin began to favor the phrase "years from now" and see that, in fact, people were wearing their futures on their sleeves, or even someplace more obvious—it just took looking at people the right way. He felt unsettled, though, walking through the cold halls of the school, feeling the exerted pressure of their futures around him, tightening the air. Sometimes when he was certain he would be re-vealed to be a fake, a total liar, he asked himself why he had ever bothered entertaining the lie to begin with.

One morning, Rafe, a freshman boy with a snaggletooth who was new to the school and generally unnoticed came to Gavin crying. Gavin was walking up a flight of stairs when he heard those soft sobs behind him, and turned to see the boy's small eyes watering with tears, and he had stopped even though it disrupted the flow of other students.

"You were right," Rafe said.

Gavin didn't even remember what he'd told Rafe, but he leaned in for a hug, assuming the worst.

"I know," Gavin said, then turned and disappeared into the crowd.

———

It was a large boat, cream with golden lines circling the hull, adorned by an enormous white sail waving slowly in the breeze. Gavin regarded it from a distance, pinched with excitement, as Jay followed. He considered reaching to hold Jay by the waist but decided not to, focusing instead on the hot summer day around him, the sweet smell of salt chalking the air, the gulls moving in slow orbit overhead.

"It's a friend's boat, to be honest," Lou said. He was dressed in bright red shorts, a beige button-down short-sleeve shirt, and sunglasses—an overthought outfit, Gavin thought.

"It's great," Gavin heard Jay say from behind.

"How far out are we going?" Gavin asked, walking up the wooden ramp.

"We're thinking of docking on the Vineyard," Louise said. She had already boarded and looked elegant, relaxed, up there in her wide hat. She leaned against the railing, and Gavin saw Lou watching her, so obviously, publicly smitten. "Some great swimming," she added, "if you're up for it."

When Gavin went to college away from home, in Pennsylvania, he had quietly resolved to become truthful. But the simple question *Where are you from?* was met with compulsive duplicity: Arizona. A small town in Kentucky. Just down the street, actually, he once said, and hated himself for it.

Even as he felt a fresh shame, the fear he had not yet

come to realize as fear was laid bare before him: It didn't matter where he was; it didn't matter what he wanted. He couldn't stop.

Sometimes, when he needed to get away from his roommate, Gavin would walk to the observation deck of the gym pool. He liked the string of colorful flags over the water, the view of the diving boards, and often took homework there, made the space his secret. Once, he had shown up during a meet and decided to stay, among those families, and watched men with abs visible from that distance, faces half masked by goggles, in competition that Gavin thought looked more like beautiful synchronicity. A kind of dance.

One of the moms turned to Gavin and asked him who he was there supporting. He instinctively chose the hottest man out on his block, pointing at him, ascribing him an intimacy: "close friend." After Gavin left, a chill ran up his spine, imagining if that woman had come to "support" his "friend." He felt queasy about it until he ate, then forgot about it, and sometimes remembered when he was back alone in that space, wondering what he'd look like in the water from that distance, and who might be there, cheering him on. He couldn't think of a single person who would. Fifteen minutes before closing, the lights in the observation deck would click off, his reflection in the dark glass startled back at him, his long, thin legs. Once he wore a hat, and the light from the pool cut half his face in darkness. He thought it made him look as if he were wearing goggles, waiting for the sharp whistle in his ear.

———————

They stopped near the tip of a dock that stretched nearly a half mile out. The rest of the boats sat lazily in the bay, jazz music playing off the bow of one in the distance, the ferry gone, the whole beach vacant except for a few small dinghies tipped on their sides. The water reflected the sun in a harsh white shimmer, and every few minutes a long, full breeze swept across the water.

The small talk from the Cape had been in turns enjoyable and unbearable for Gavin. The heat irritated him as Lou had poured them glasses of red wine and relaxed, talking about the weather, plans for the holidays. Gavin wanted for Jay to say something, to prove his forethought aloud, but Jay only sat and occasionally sipped from his glass, the wine staining his upper lip a line of dark purple. The silence seemed polite to Gavin, and an instant later, it struck him as rude. Then it changed back. He couldn't figure out which was true.

"It's a beautiful spot, isn't it?" Louise said.

"It's very nice," Lou added, taking off his shirt. A sweaty fuzz of gray hair slicked his back, and Gavin flinched at the sight. But then there was the splash and mist of Lou jumping in, and Louise preparing to go in after him. The amount of fun they were having seemed, to Gavin, to border on caricature.

Gavin moved closer to Jay, sitting so close next to him that he could see the slight raised bump above his eye, tan concealer over the purple, in a way he felt would force Jay to either take his hand or acknowledge an active decision not to. But Jay only looked forward, past him, at the island rippled with trees swaying in the calm breeze, the warm day.

"This is so nice," Jay said. The moment felt avoided to Gavin. He felt the tart wine in his stomach, the warm air made invincibly calm around him. He wanted to prove something to Jay, to seal his lie into truth while he still could. He stood and walked to the side of the boat. Louise and Lou were treading water, their arms moving in wide, practiced arcs. Gavin lifted his shirt over his head, making a point not to turn toward Jay.

It was true he had lied about being a professional diver in order to level what he had then considered a physical difference he couldn't reconcile—how, he often thought, could a guy like that like a guy like him? He had this thought even despite the beautiful moments they'd shared, the proof he had lived that Jay really did like him and (despite frequent skepticism) really might love him. But Gavin had made that monster lurk under them both, a shark tearing through deep water at the trace of blood, the rows of teeth they could not escape.

Gavin wasn't out of shape, but his chest sagged slightly. When he thought of his body, he thought of the moment when he emerged from the shower, turning away from his reflection in the steamed mirror.

He aligned his toes against the edge of the boat, steadied his breathing, and briefly imagined himself as Jay saw him. The thought pushed him forward and up, arcing down slow into the bright water. Unlike that day he had dived without thinking, he put great effort into what he imagined was excellent diving technique. But as his face hit the surface, he had taken in a breath, accidentally—pressure pinched the bridge of his nose, and the water tickled his throat, he coughed, and then there was the cold water in his mouth, and he was choking. He couldn't control his arms, and through his panic it occurred to him how strange he must have looked.

What Gavin remembered next: Jay's hands over his ribs, his legs finally working to tread water, unable to breathe without coughing, the terrified, childish look on Lou's face, which bobbed on the surface feet away, Jay's warm body suddenly pressed up behind him, and Louise asking from what seemed like a great distance, "Is he all right? Is he *okay*?"

Gavin's future would surprise him: after leaving Jay and moving to another state, he would fall in love with a polite and quiet biology teacher, and later settle in a small town in upstate New York, where he would walk daily to a pond a half mile from their home. He would go there early in the morning, when the fog lifted off the water with an ethereal shine, and the years would melt around him to reveal the memory of that moment at Black Lake: the sun slanting down in a single cutting ray, the thud of his labored breathing in that boat, the silver whistle swinging from the lifeguard's neck, the held breath of everything as Brady choked out that first living sound. The pond would be the only body of water for miles, which Gavin would enjoy. Some spring mornings the fog would come down from the mountains to meet the mist at the water's edge, and when it did, it gave Gavin the impression of entering a dream—or, he sometimes thought, of finally waking from one.

SIGNS

When I arrive at the cliffs, they've been cordoned off, dotted with small orange cones. Someone tried to climb them and fell. "Wet moss," a construction worker tells me. "No one believes the signs."

Everyone believes the signs, I almost say, *except the few who don't*. I also almost ask if they've found the body. I am decidedly too interested, but being a tourist does that to you. Everything becomes a riddle to crack.

"What's that?" he asks. He points to the small blue jar of my friend's ashes, glinting with sunlight in my left hand.

"Nothing," I say.

We discuss the weather, and I tell him that I'm headed to Amsterdam. The day could not be more beautiful, all smiling strangers. Pink flowers nodding in the tall grass. His words are low and light, easily dismissed.

RORSCHACH

There's never been a line at the Boston Opera House in the morning, not for the seven years I've been turning on the lights, but today people are lined down the block, huddled in small groups, their breath white in the frozen air. It's opening night for the Crucifixion. Nobody wants a bad seat.

New York and Chicago have already started their Crucifixions, and people are flying in from all over the country to see them. *No two shows are alike!* the posters read, a black fingerprint behind the text, but that's not exactly true. The whole thing is scripted, except for the nailing itself—no one's sure how that will play out, though we got the regulation hammer and spikes last week. The past few days, I could hear Tuck and Andy—the guys cast as the Roman guards—outside my door, knocking the dull tips of the spikes into the wood, practicing.

At first, the Crucifixions weren't that popular. People were hesitant to see this sort of thing, and many would leave at intermission. But it didn't take long for the interview series to start, for criminals to say they preferred this to the electric chair. It's all volunteer, but there doesn't seem to be any shortage of Jesuses in the high-security prisons. Our show's run ends when we stop making money, or whenever I say so—the benefit of producing.

I unlock the theater door, a thick gold lock that reminds me, in its beauty, what a great job I have, and close the doors behind me. I walk down the left aisle like I always do, checking to make sure there's no trash in the seats. In a few hours, the cast will arrive, followed by the crew, then the night's star, Alix Hoffman, forty-six, of Worcester, who pleaded guilty to first-degree murder two years ago. But for now, the air is still and thin, quiet. The ghost light in the proscenium has taken a different shine this morning, its faint glow some terrible omen.

"It doesn't look like anything," I told my friend Noah. "Like, a bug. A swatted fly."

The Rorschach test was the last in a series of attempts at divining what, exactly, was wrong with me—or, that's what I assumed. The final vestige of a friend group I had when I moved to the city, Noah was the sort of guy who felt his undergrad psychology degree entitled him to judge strangers from across crowded bars with an accuracy that was really just stubbornness, a kind of no-second-look sensibility that once seemed wise and now just felt pitiable. We'd practiced with less formal methods of healing, everything from crystals I kept in a plastic bag to powder I was supposed to mix into water and then leave on my bedside table.

("But do not drink that," he'd cautioned sternly, without explanation.) My night terrors were growing more vivid, cripplingly real; I wasn't sleeping more than a few hours each night, and even then, the sleep was irregular. I would have seen a real therapist, but this was one way of trying to get Noah to fall back in love with me—if he ever even had been to begin with—and it made him feel useful, which gave the profoundly misguided impression for both of us that this face time was working.

"Look again," Noah said.

I looked again. In the dream I'd been having for the last two weeks, I sit with my mother watching a magician pull calico cats from his sleeve, levitate chairs, whistle into being a string of Christmas lights over the audience. At one point, two women wheel a coffin to the center of the stage, and the magician asks for a volunteer—this is the moment I become terrified—and my mother walks to the stage and steps into the box, which is then closed and sawed through its center. When the time comes for the reveal, it hasn't worked. She's been halved. But the audience still applauds.

"It seriously looks like someone shit on a piece of paper," I told Noah.

We moved through the inkblots quickly, and I nearly saw things in each: the almost-head of a man, a near-crab with its pincers defensively raised. ("You really don't need to be that specific," he'd said of that detail.) When we finished, Noah placed the papers on his desk, then turned back to me. From his puzzled expression, I knew that, like me, he hadn't figured anything out.

"These don't seem to be helping?" he said.

"No," I said. "I'm not really sick." There was a fine line to walk between needing his guidance and seeming well enough to be datable. But I had no way of knowing that I wasn't sick, no way of knowing what then might have been my worst fear, if I'd been paying attention: that my conscience would rise up in me months later after agreeing to cast the Crucifixion, after watching a man die months afterward upstage left, feet from where Hansel and Gretel had become trapped only days prior, next to a cauldron filled with dry ice.

"How does that make you feel?" Noah asked. "That you don't feel sick."

I gave him an old look—what a stupid question. A little mean, but I excused it. I hoped my intelligence hurt him. I was the one who got into graduate school and moved out of his parents' basement, even if studying late into the night had cost me things nothing would ever cost him. Walking down the library steps at midnight a few months into dating, I could feel his loss of interest in just the way he had held my hand. Intuition I tried to shake but prophesized that disaster, when days later he broke the news to me in that same library. He said that he had "lost the feeling." I missed hearing this at first and had to ask, knowing from the apology in his eyes what was happening, for him to repeat himself. Staying there, next to those books, felt like a way never to leave the moment, a space that would grant me the chance to turn back to the start if only I figured out how. My demeanor changed and never changed back. I became the kind of person I had until then hated, who dealt out bullshit pushback, my resentment like an outfit I selected and wore every day, until the clothes were my skin, and I was my job, my current starring role as a producer. I had wished it all up, even the heartbreak. The curse of my intuition, I sometimes joke to myself, though of course it is no joke.

Not even two months of dating Noah, and over a decade later his was the spell I couldn't shake. He lit candles on the table between us at the start of each session, and I was back in his apartment, the berry smell of his hair, those old posters on his old apartment walls showing off an interest in vintage horror movies I always knew would never last.

"So you know, reliably, the dream won't end well," he said. "Have you ever tried stopping it?"

"Is there science behind this stuff? To be honest, that sounds really dumb," I told him, which was true. He laughed and it made my heart jump, voiding my irritation at his seeming not to have listened when I said, several meetings ago, that I can't move in it.

"I can't move in it," I said again, as if for the first time.

Noah had flipped to a new page of his yellow notebook, scribbling. Once, when he excused himself to the bathroom where he indulged a long fart, I glimpsed an open page; it read: M 7–7, TR full, F 12–8. His nursing shifts. Information I did not want to have. I imagined him helpful instead, reducing my life to bones and what those might be: *antidepressants, weight gain, anxiety, mother's death.*

"I'm going to ask," he said, "that you try to stop your dream. Just tonight. And that you note how that goes."

"I'll try," I said. The homework was a promise of another

weird half hour with Noah. When I went to put it on my calendar, not that I was at risk of forgetting it, I saw that word: *date!*

Something's wrong with the cross, or at least that's what Tuck—in full makeup—is telling me an hour before the curtain rises, like someone who doesn't want to keep his job.

"It's just wobbling," he says. "A bit. Like, only a little."

"Crosses don't wobble," I say.

I can hear the protesters' chant through my office window: "Respect Christ! Respect our Lord!" That it doesn't rhyme assuages my fear these people might be under good leadership. Thankfully, there aren't nearly as many as on New York's opening night just over a year ago: riots in the streets outside the off-Broadway theater, cars tipped and set ablaze, tall white candles lit in vigil, the whole scene mournful and angry.

The idea for the production had come from two brothers, a pastor and a prison guard with a passion for community theater, the latter of whom got it in his mind, walking past death row inmates one day, what a live-action crucifixion might look like. Next thing you know, the guys have an article in the local paper that goes viral with controversy, and CNN brings it to air: these two brothers talking about whether this could happen. How? The ratings climb, and everyone gets interested. "We just don't live in those times anymore," one anchor had said, laughing uncomfortably. Which is how my colleague Ethan took notice, hungover,

watching a monitor at his airport terminal while waiting
for a flight home, then sending off a stray interested e-mail.
His Chicago theater had just secured *Jesus Christ Superstar*
for fall. By the time the plane had landed, he had an enthu-
siastic voicemail from both the siblings. "The rest," Ethan
told me over scotch a few months ago, looking a tired, un-
easy mess, the regret apparent through his put-on confidence, "is history."

People are getting used to the Crucifixions; the churches
that haven't closed down are the only ones funding this
sort of protest, but I'm not sure why they bother. It's all
legal and has been for a few years. After the shows, a lot of
families go out to dinner. Dates take each other for drinks.

Tuck tries everything he can think of to fix the cross—
glues it, then nails it. Finally, the boards stay.

In a dressing room, he props the cross against a wall.
Now that it's finally ready, a guard brings Alix into the
room. I was instructed to do this by Ethan, the producer
who started the first Crucifixions in Chicago. Apparently,
without instruction, one of their Jesuses had the spikes
driven through his hands, which didn't hold his body up—
he slid off the wood like peeling wallpaper. "Goddamn
understudies," Ethan told me.

The first thing I notice is: Alix is fatter than his mug
shot. By a good fifty pounds. He has a prominent hooked
nose and deep bags under his eyes; a tattoo of a thick chain
that will be hidden with foundation curls around his bicep.

If I saw him anywhere else, I'd think he was a criminal. He doesn't quite have that Prince of Peace look I was hoping for, the kind advertised on some of our flyers.

"They'll go through the wrists," Tuck says. He holds his arms out on the cross, demonstrating. "The lashing won't hurt—not real whips. We'll be quick." Even in death, in the theater, everyone has to be on the same page.

Alix backs up so his body is aligned on the cross. It reminds me of how doctors measure height during checkups. Tuck explains that Alix needs to cross his ankles once lifted onto it.

"And this. This is important." He holds up a small bottle of blue liquid, taps it with his nail. It looks like food coloring. "You know what this is, I know. Drink it right before the scene. When Mary starts crying up-left, just throw it back. Like a shot." The small bottle, shaped like a vial, is poison. It's a variety that shuts down nerve sensation, then organ function—one by one turning off the light switches of the body. I remember signing the papers for it weeks ago. The forms were stamped with special seals, coupled with confidentiality agreements and safety hazard notices. Ethan had told me it was optional, that technically I could decide whether I wanted a more realistic scene. But he said the wailing on his opening night, that fierce echo of dying noise in the wide atrium of the house, haunted him. He said the theater is a place for a lot of things, but when you get down to it, you always have to work to make it real but not too real. Under "purpose" on the supply request form, I wrote: *To aid in the realistic depiction of the final scene.* What I think I meant was: *To kill a man as painlessly as possible.*

"It's going to make you weak," Tuck adds, holding the bottle up to the light. "So be aware."

Alix nods. I haven't heard him speak, and I guess it doesn't matter—none of the Jesuses have any lines. Some critics have called this "a powerful choice to transcend literal narrative," but really it's just because we don't have much time to fill them in.

"The set is a huge crown," Tuck tells Alix on his way out. "It's thin, just supposed to cast a silhouette, so don't touch it. It could fall."

"What would be great," I say to Tuck, "is having everything not almost fall, or break."

"What would be great," Tuck says, "is getting through tonight."

It's not his place to talk to me like this, but he knows I need him too much to call him on it right now. He tightens his gold belt and gives me a look. "Here we go," he says, and Alix follows him, head bowed, out of the room.

I walk to the back of the house, which is filled to capacity. People are sitting in the aisles on the balcony. A mother and her two sons hurry toward their seats, excusing themselves as they bump against others. The lights flash, then dim. The curtain flinches and begins to rise.

"May I have a volunteer?"

The magician was tall and thin, skeletal, with long arms and slick black hair. When the light caught his face, I noticed he had the just-left-of-handsome look of someone I'd briefly dated a few months ago and also still not gotten over, who broke up with me on a date by gently noting an apparently obvious lack of chemistry—a guy I since had tried to forget by way of just hoping I would forget him eventually.

My mother and I were sitting at one of dozens of small, round tables at the back of an old theater. The night's first act had been astonishing—leaf petals summoned from the stage's wings, hovering midair like birds frozen in flight, before vanishing without sound. I was starting to feel anxious. We were sitting in the back, the old proscenium illuminated softly, as if with only peripheral light. The room smelled like cigar smoke, though no one was smoking.

"You!" the magician said, beckoning with his hand. "In the back." He was calling my mother.

Suddenly, I came to; I remembered Noah and what he'd said, and how the goal was to stop this, to put an end to it. As I realized this, I became anchored in place by some familiar force—fear? Anxiety? Whatever the thing was, it only stilled my body. I watched as my mother shook the magician's hand and climbed into the box. As he began to saw, I thought to myself: *I can will this not to happen. I can change the ending.*

When the box separated—the two women carefully opening each half to face out—I realized I had, in fact, revised the dream. The audience applauded and the magician bowed slowly. She was gone.

Twenty minutes in, and I make a tentative note to fire the entire sound crew. Feedback is ruining beats. King Herod's lines are dropped, and he feigns fury at the thought of not being heard; he's a real pro and gets a lot of laughs. If no one knew what was coming, if no one considered this merely an opening act, I'd guess some people would walk out.

Miguel, the technical director, races down the stairs. I can tell he's been looking for me.

"The cross," he says, short of breath. "Will Alix stay?"

He's a small Mexican man with a thick Australian accent and bad acne scarring, the kind of person with a history I wouldn't believe if I heard it. I hired him a few months ago because he had designed for an off-Broadway production of *Les Mis* and seemed agreeable—a trait I've grown to loathe. I now recognize he's just feckless.

"Isn't that your job, to know that?"

"I didn't order the crosses."

I can hear Herod make his exit: loud and dramatic. The audience reels with laughter, but it's muted through the walls.

"Figure it out," I say. "You need to make it happen."

I imagine Alix sliding off the cross, not fully dead. I imagine refunds and complaints, bad reviews. Miguel rushes back up the stairs, his tiny legs scissoring up the steps in annoying bursts. I put my hands in my pockets and focus on my breathing. I fix my hair, looking at my reflection in the dark glass of the door, and wait for intermission.

"So you stopped it," Noah said, uncrossing his legs. He lit a small white candle and placed it carefully on the table between us. Romance, suddenly, like I'd fallen into a trick room. "That's good."

"I didn't stop it. I think I just changed it."

We couldn't agree on what I'd done to "fix" the dream. And that question haunted me, a second ghost: How could I even know if I'd been the one to manage it? Were there ever really answers, or did we just decide on our version of the truth, cling to it until we found another?

Noah had his yellow notebook not on his desk but on his lap, which I took as some kind of sign he felt the meeting was especially crucial or telling. I wanted to read what he was writing, to learn if he was, in fact, making new, essential judgments. If he was just writing his work schedule. Or if he was merely learning what I consider obvious: that I will run back to a memory to make sure I haven't just dreamed it all up myself. If I was pathetic to him, I agreed with the assessment, the diagnosis, whatever it was. I was.

Noah put the pen in the crease of the notebook, then closed it and placed it on his desk. He leaned back in his chair, taking something in. It seemed like a move he would have done in college, just before making a stupid point with impressive confidence. I wanted to hand him a paper with a grade for this mock job he was doing—C+.

"So, what are we talking about today?" I asked.

"I want to talk about whatever you do," he said.

This was his way of admitting he couldn't care less what I had to say, and we both knew it. Each time Noah deferred to me, I experienced it as an admission of his stupidity. He wanted gossip. Like everyone, he wanted to know what really happened on that car ride home from Christmas Eve Mass, his ears perking up as if it were the only car crash to ever occur in Boston, the only car to hit another car on an interstate off-ramp. The full scene I couldn't cast, even to myself. After Noah had read the obituary, he'd shown back up in my life, a rescue operation—*I'm still here!* his presence seemed to say. At first only part of me wondered if he was in it for the gossip, and I became convinced this was true because I wanted it to be.

One night, alone in my apartment, I wrote about what had happened in great detail: the sudden glare of two headlights turning to face me seconds before the uncanny crack of something (her neck?), which sounded like a beer being opened, something I learned the next day when I tried to do exactly that and dropped the bottle, from the instinctual memory of the noise, onto the kitchen tile. The white mist of smoke rising like a last breath from the hood of the car, and the way I had for only a moment looked up from the wheel to see the frost sparkling across the entire windshield, like a static channel, waiting for it to change. After I finished writing, I read the first paragraph and felt ill. I deleted everything and began to cry. I learned I didn't really know what happened, except she died on impact and I sat there like an idiot rubbing my sore wrist, whining, swearing at this drunk fuck in the obscene night for a good three minutes.

"The inkblots," I told him. "I want to try them again."

"Okay," he said, and lifted them off the table.

I took each slowly, considered the careful, ugly symmetry. The shapes began, almost magically, to snap into place: a jaw, two women's faces, a lion's mane. I turned to look at Noah, to see how well I was doing. He flipped the blot and squinted, looking for the mane.

"I can't quite see it," he said. The candle flickered between us, as if to announce a ghost. "But as you know, there's no wrong answer. They all kind of look like manes, huh?"

There's a moment of silence that the great shows and bombing ones share, a kind of piercing stillness that briefly eclipses even the show itself, when no lines are being said— a beat that washes over the audience and actors. At first, standing outside the theater, hearing nothing, I think something's gone wrong. But as I open the door—carefully, to avoid drawing attention—I see Alix walking across the stage, apostles in tow. A soft red hue is cast on the scrim, the director's not-so-subtle touch at foreshadowing that I reminded her on several occasions didn't need to happen; people know how the story ends.

Alix is wearing a loincloth, his soft belly noticeable even from where I stand. The group is just walking, stage left to stage right, wing to wing. I can faintly hear their steps on the ground.

An older woman a few rows from the back is choking up, and a man shushes her from behind.

The next scene arrives—Judas's monologue on the thrust—but the theater has taken on a chill, the whole audience sharing one brutal, fascinated awareness: The man they just saw walk across the stage will be put to death before them. I realize what I'd have known if I'd seen the full production before, why the Crucifixions have been tanking the new blockbuster-hopeful musicals and putting whole playhouses out of business, why Los Angeles and Atlanta and Seattle are hurrying the paperwork with their prisons. It's breathtaking.

I had decided to stop seeing Noah, a choice that I told myself was an act of self-respect but was really just a dramatic move to get him to acknowledge something, anything, so that I might find in that acknowledgment the truth about the depth of his feeling toward me. Desperation upon desperation, a story I knew well.

Nothing was helping the anxiety, and the dreams were persistent—it turned out I had changed the ending, but I could never stop it entirely. The women would turn to open the halved coffin, the hinges swinging open with a woody thud to reveal an empty space. But because Noah had brought in more inkblots, I felt obligated to indulge him, just one last time. I planned to ask about the yellow book, about his notes, to learn how he saw me, if he ever even had, but I wasn't sure how to, and so I never did.

"Mermaid," I said, noting the vague silhouetted outline of a flipper. He held up a new page. "Willow tree."

I had stopped trying to see exactly the things in the ink and looked instead for semblances, shapes. When you lowered your expectations, there were a lot more options for what something might be. I found myself, when I closed my eyes between blots, back at that table in the library, the blue light from the windows on my hand, waiting with moronic hope to hear his footsteps back up that marble staircase. For him to say that he'd had the kind of epiphany I wouldn't have believed even then. That he was wrong.

During intermission, women wept in the bathroom, moved. Men formed small groups in the lobby, discussing a blizzard in the forecast, their work, how they expected Alix would be crucified *exactly*, down to the kind of nail, the technique of the swinging arm. Miguel informed me, unconvincingly, that he'd fixed the cross, and I told him I'd believe him when I saw it.

Now, everyone is back in their seats. It's the scene before the crucifixion. Lepers are hobbling down the aisles, shaking, holding their wounds, asking for a pittance. People are leaning away from them. I remember talking to Ethan about this scene, and why it preceded the crucifixion, because it confused me: Why have a dozen actors in full hair and makeup and costume wasted on these few minutes? And his response was something like, "To freak them out, and then freak them out more. To unsettle them, physically, then mentally. It's what they're paying for, really." And I guess I agree. They're getting what they paid for.

I walk back to the lobby. Outside, several protesters drink coffee from paper cups, sit on the curb. Their few signs are propped against a trash can. I turn around, because I don't want them to see me, not that they'd know who I am if they did.

I sit on the steps and listen to my heartbeat, which has started to pick up. Pontius Pilate's voice is all I can hear, his side of the conversation, and through the intensity of the moment, I consider how I'll deal with the sound crew. The words firing out from the stage: "Are you? Well, are you?"

There's a beat coming I've seen before, heard before, when Herod is the first to shout: "Crucify him!" And then it really starts. The whole thing picks up, gets manic. Even the rehearsals got heated. I try to imagine how it's going to work, whether Alix will struggle at all, whether he's really prepared to die—something I hadn't actually considered before.

Herod kills the line, and I jump at it, even though I expect it. There's a cry in the audience, someone is having a fit, and an usher escorts the woman to the lobby. Her sweater is tight against her, and her skin has begun to sag slightly with age. Her stomach pulses with each shallow breath. Her purse is wrapped around her shoulder, and a loose tissue falls to the floor as she blows her nose. She looks up at me and then back down. I think I hear her say, "I'm sorry," through the choke of a sob, but I'm not sure, and she leaves the building.

The scene onstage unfolds rapidly, hysterically, and though I can only hear it, my heart seems to keep time to it.

For minutes, I sit. When the frenzy calms, after Alix has been nailed to the cross, after Miguel gives me the thumbs-up from the top of the stairs—a gesture I take to mean Alix is secure—I open the door to the theater. All is silent. I press the oak carefully, mindful of its hinges, until I see the stage, the backs of countless heads before it, the marley thinly glossed with blood, the enormous silhouette of the thorny crown behind the scrim, which is backlit with strong red light. But even when I look closely, I can't see the crown—not exactly. I concentrate on the shape, the perfect mirror of its form. I wait for it to snap into being, to know the ending I've made. Someone says, "My God," and I realize I've forgotten if this is how the show ends. Or if there are more lines. If someone missed their cue. If someone isn't listening.

GOLDFISH BOWL

wo hours before I tell him it's over, a man I'm dating holds the holy water above the goldfish bowl. He says, "What happens—ha-ha—if I pour this in?"

I say, "Shut up."

It's a game we play. He says anything and I'm rude to him.

In its bowl, the goldfish already looks dead, its fins losing their color. The goldfish is sick with something called dropsy. I got it a few weeks ago after moving six states west to start a new life in a town where no one knows that it is possible to test positive in your mother's bathroom two months after a night you don't remember. I moved to tell the world I am happy now—I *am* happy now!—but the problem is I don't think the world believes it yet.

The idea was the goldfish would make me less lonely. Then its abdomen swelled like an egg and weighed it down, where it now rests on the gravel.

"Something's wrong with it," he says. He does one of his ha-has again. "Maybe this will cure it."

He tips the bottle, smiling, and asks me again what would

happen. I detect he comes from the sort of family that easily forgives bad behavior like this. What I want to say is I don't know. The water is my mother's. She's hundreds of miles northeast watching our dog sleep. A little respect, please.

Instead, I say, "Put it down. Don't waste it on a fish."

DIVING, DRIFTING

Emma watched from her hotel balcony each morning as the local kids spearfished: stingrays, snappers, the occasional hogfish, each one split through with one immense stick, then hollowed out, and thrown to boil on the colorless sand. The children scattered the length of the beach and into its narrower lagoons, surfacing only to showcase their prized kills. Emma first pretended not to notice, but the animals' blood lit up in loose pockets along the coast, followed by throngs of seabirds flying above them. She noted those areas most heavily harvested, where the water settled to a pink, translucent mist, and resolved not to wade near them, aware she'd want one evening swim. She was taken by the sight, and the movement gave her something to think about.

Emma's father had passed, and the hotel was all she could afford in the coastal South Carolina suburb, a series of cul-de-sacs knotted into one neighborhood. Her mother had told her she was to stay for the wake and nothing else. *And how would they feel? A dyke at a funeral. Just come, then leave.* It had all happened quickly and over the phone, which wasn't to say Emma hadn't been hurt by it. She'd heard it before—the slurs, the dog jokes, the word "butch" a rare, kind offering—and for as long as she could remember her family's words had defined her. Her father was no different, but he loved the ocean as she did, and that was all that kept the relationship tolerable—frequent visits to the pier, where their moods seemed to jointly lift with the tide.

Sometimes Emma had dreams in which her mother was a shark and she was a dolphin. She never slept through them. There was something about how each of the sharks had smiles that made them different. The difference was in their eyes too. When she was near the ocean, the dreams intensified. And on the morning of the wake, one boy caught a sand shark and slid it ashore, pitched through the mouth, thick stems of blood trailing through the bright water. Emma leaned on the balcony's precarious fencing, listening for the noise she came to expect.

The only girl on the beach bold enough to mingle with the cluster of ten-year-old boys was a tomboy. She bent down and poked the fish a little, her hair matted and thick beneath an embroidered black baseball cap. It was Emma, at fourteen, with curlier hair and a tighter, sweeter voice.

The boy had plans for the shark—it was clear from the way he hauled it back to shore—but Emma could see his disappointment at its size, its pathetic lank, shriveled to just another fish. The young girl wrapped fists around the spear, twisted, popped it from its hold on the shark. Scooping it into her arms, she shifted it toward the ocean. She nudged its fins, let it go. Its carcass tugged against the waves, rolled with their corkscrewed funnels, turned pallid and a bit sideways. The band of kids watched as it clotted the water in one massive stain.

A few of the boys turned to the girl, her awkward, shifting weight, and appeared to laugh. Emma couldn't hear them—complimentary breakfast was about to be served in the hotel's enormous atrium, the noisiest morning she'd seen since college—but there was no mistaking the boys' amusement. The girl ripped off her baseball cap and ran back to her parents, who were positioned somewhere on the main beach, but Emma's eyes grew tired as she tried to follow the girl through the puzzling mess of umbrellas and beach balls and other children. She reclined on the couch, taking in the forecasted weather. "One sunny day ahead," chimed the weatherman. Emma slouched, then corrected her posture. She hadn't mapped her way to the funeral home yet, and she began to wonder if seeing her father— his jaw square and stiff, though without its signature twitch—would be worth it at all. The prospect of an open casket kept her where she was.

The wake formally began a half hour after Emma started showering. She opted to miss the ceremony completely, as if it were a menu option. The rest of the day seemed to pull away from her—first slowly, then rapidly, as if reined taut by some colossal sea monster. As night settled around the hotel, Emma gathered her belongings and made her way down the fourteen flights of stairs. As she walked the length of the beach, void of any locals in the night, she noted one purse, inlaid with delicate patchwork, partially hidden by sand.

Emma examined it from a few feet, then a few inches, and tipped its mouth open. Every few moments she paused and looked about her surroundings, ready to recognize anything other than the ocean or the occasional scuttle of hermit crabs at her feet. She began to leaf through its contents—the dim parking lot light spilling with velvet serenity toward the beach—noting: lipstick, a few tarnished bracelets, blank postcards, a ripped photo of some unrecognizable statue in Europe. As Emma became more fascinated by a new tropical-peach flavor of sugarless gum, a woman's voice peeped from behind her.

"Excuse me? Miss?"

"Sorry!" Emma started. "I'm sorry."

She began shoveling what she had laid out on the sand around her back into the woman's purse. The woman's features were delicate, her hair sleek and conditioned beneath a fancy hat, one Emma would never wear because it looked like an oversize doily, but which suited the woman just fine.

"Oh no. It's my fault, leaving it on this beach." The woman's embarrassment seemed to radiate from her.

"Are you kidding? This is totally my fault. I'm so nosy. I'm so sorry."

Emma handed the woman her bag.

"There you go. And, sorry."

Emma paced back toward her hotel room, up the flights of stairs, fumbling on herself, filled with nauseating self-pity. Reaching her door, she realized she had left her green and white towel next to the woman's precious purse. Exploring the panoramic view from her balcony, she couldn't chart its location on the beach. The air had staled to a breezy pulp. Lights flashed from the lot, ebbing with the darkness before pulling out and veering onto the interstate.

Three voicemails had been left by her mother. She deleted each one separately, indulging in their gradual departure from her phone. The waves outside seemed louder than Emma remembered them moments ago. Something in the water leapt, then fell back in—tasting the air for a short moment, and wishing again for water.

The next morning, Emma woke from her most vivid nightmare: she, a dolphin, her mother, a shark, and her father, an enormous spear. She couldn't understand how she knew these things were so. She and her mother were caught in a gigantic, rectangular aquarium, taking bites from each other, while a spear pitched from the water's surface at desultory angles, holing them through the torso and dorsal fins, marking them in ruby, graphed lines, as if both were nothing more than pincushions. Emma vowed to attempt this retelling at her next week's therapy session.

Beach activity slowed as winds from the north grew stronger. Still, the girl and only two other boys played on the temperate beach. Emma watched as the girl and boy buried the shortest child in a pit and filled it with sand, leaving only his head peeking above the surface. The two continued to play for a time, then grew restless, exhausting all their options for fun in the feigned disembodiment. Both began to trek through clouds of seaweed in search of small shells and stones to skip. The boy struggled to free himself from the sand, and before long the eldest was throwing sand at the girl, while the girl hurled handfuls of pebbles back at him, and an adult came to dig up the smallest. The girl escaped to the jetty, balancing on a rock the shape of an arrowhead, testing how far she could slip without falling.

Emma returned to her television. Her phone had accumulated two new voicemails: one from her mother, and one from the first woman to break her heart, who had done so during a five-hour call, which had occurred through the same phone. Both were deleted simultaneously. There was nothing acceptable about either the phone calls or messages.

The weatherman announced, "Hurricane Lisa confirmed to be headed for Northern Florida." He paused a bit, receiving further word from his lagging prompt. "Its trajectory up until now has been unknown. Keep an eye out for updates."

Breakfast was served in the atrium per usual, and Emma decided to attend, since she had nothing better to do. She avoided the dairy and bacon but indulged in extravagant portions of bread and fresh fruit. Her therapist had told her that eating healthier food could erase the cells that stimulated her strange nightmares. And though Emma didn't like pineapple, the possibility of a restful night had her clearing her plate.

That night, Emma headed to the beach, hoping the water might cool her skin, which had begun to burn up through the afternoon. And it did assuage it. But eventually, the ocean began to roll too quickly, the waves piled on top of one another—choppy and growing in the roiling surf. Emma walked from the water and, soaked, returned to her room, footprinting pockets of sand into the gaudily ornate carpet. Silently, she cursed herself for not purchasing another towel.

After showering, she curled into bed, her conscience spinning about the room, blaring in and out of focus with the weather report, the television monitor.

Two hours later, she woke. Not from dreams or nightmares, but the storm. Outside, the ocean churned restlessly, a few beachside homes nearly ripped from their thin foundations, wooden planks visible beneath. The hotel's generator had kicked in, a groan emanating throughout the building. Trees knocked against the hotel's crenellated roof, wind uprooted shrubs and flew them downtown in broad strokes. Emma reached for her phone, which held in it one voicemail. She flipped it open and pressed it against her ear, which was red from the sickness, the stress, the storm.

"And one more thing, Emma," the familiarly shrill voice spat. "They say it's a category four. It's getting stronger. Just leave."

Emma looked out onto the balcony, past the beach, toward Hilton Head, which earlier reports had said would receive tremendous impact, despite its distance from the eye of the storm. Something about the Gulf Stream. After a few hours, Emma found rhythm in the tumultuousness of the weather—the melodic snapping of twigs, the itching of sand in the air—and fell asleep.

She woke before dawn, her nightmare having stolen the little sleep she had been able to endure. Another omen. But there were no sharks in her dream. No dolphins or spears either. Instead, Emma had dreamt she was a little girl, chasing boys on a beach. And when she caught one, he would turn around and his face would be her father's face. From the jaw to the hairline, her father's features, almost painted on. Or maybe she was chasing her father in a boy's body. The dream embarrassed her, and she made a commitment not to tell her therapist. He was only interested in hearing about Lucy—the famed, failed lesbian flash romance—anyway. He said it had a lot to do with her slumping posture and lack of self-confidence.

From breakfast, Emma noticed commotion outside. The storm had subsided completely by midmorning, having taken a sudden, southern turn. Dozens of people gathered as the waves tamed themselves, combing the beach for residual treasure, anything the storm had deposited in its wake. Emma looked for conch shells, but none interrupted her diligent search. She pocketed a few sea stars the size of her fingernail and continued walking south. She imagined herself lazy then, chasing a storm she never wanted to catch.

The little girl appeared behind Emma, then raced forward, past her, stamping her feet in the incoming tide. She looked nervous, and was holding something Emma couldn't make out. Peeking behind a jetty, the girl disappeared, then reappeared moments later. Emma knew instantly: She had buried something. The tide rose and took back what the storm and the people did not wish to keep. The little girl continued searching for shells as Emma returned to pack her belongings for her flight back to Michigan that night.

Before her final evening swim, Emma located the patch of sand in which the girl had placed her treasure. Gracelessly stubbing her toe on an outcropping in the rock, she began to paw through the ground. It was buried deep, as if she had experience with this sort of thing, aware that depth would keep things from washing ashore. It was the baseball cap, tattered along the edges, stitched with cursive; the words *Happy 7th, Ruby* were scratched inside. Emma left it there, in the space between low and high tide, so that the ocean might take it, or Ruby might, if she changed her mind.

Part III

WHO I AM

MASTER'S THESIS

While I'm taking off the mud mask in my bathroom mirror, Brad leaves me a voicemail saying he has a "big idea," and it concerns me into meeting him. It turns out the big idea is this: He's going to throw all his childhood stuff into the ocean. No, he's going to burn it—one big flaming pile. Or dump it off a cliff, drop it from a flying helicopter. He's going to get rid of it, no question, but what would make for the best shot?

"Also," he adds, "can I use your things too?"

The tide has receded, exposing a muddy lip of damp sand. We sit a few feet from the lifeguard watch, which feels fitting, as if I heard that voicemail as a whistle. It's just us, thank God. This is his master's thesis, he explains. It can't be some "cheap stunt."

I think, those are exactly the words.

Back in middle school in Vermont, Brad was the only other gay person I knew, or, I thought I knew. But we're grown now—"forty-somethings," he's started saying, in that uncomfortably ambiguous way. We've been with too many feckless men, talked about giving up too much to be doing this. We're too old to be burning our shit or littering in the ocean.

"Or," Brad asks, "are we just old enough?"

"Too old," I say. I draw the vague outline of a mermaid's tail in the sand.

"What's that?" he asks.

"A cock," I say.

"It doesn't look like a cock."

"Sure it does."

"Well what's *that*, then?"

"What's what?"

He hesitates. "Your wrists." I put two wrists under his face, like I'm being handcuffed, for his inspection. He now knows the question offends me, like he still thinks I'm Old Ken, who called him with my bare feet on the edge of that cold bridge, like *he*'s the one taking care of me at 5 a.m., talking *me* off the ledge over a voicemail I ignored. Confronting the moment always kills it, and I can't tell him I'm fine now because that will clinch his belief I'm not. My outsize mistrust of him is one way of winning, and my awareness of it makes me feel smarter than him. He looks away from my wrists and back out at the sea, and I'm relieved he won't try to drag the interrogation on. I want to fire back by asking about the size of his loans for this project. Is he even thinking about the future?

"Sorry. Anyway," he says, "I think it'd be good for us. Healthy."

This gets me: Brad talking about healthy. Even before

he got sick, he was the kind of guy to get up at three in the morning and drive two hours just to "say hi" to a man he was dating, the kind of guy who lied to strangers about where he was from ("We have coconuts just like these in Bora Bora." "Sir, these are jackfruit."). Through his skeletal frame, in his glassy eyes, he believed, and still believes, if I'm seeing him right, that things will turn out well if only you follow your instinct, your dumb, hurt heart.

"That doesn't sound healthy," I say.

"We hated that part of our life, right?"

"Maybe," I say. "Who knows! I forget."

"We did, we hated it." He draws a pair of balls on my mermaid tail.

We each wait for the other person to speak; it creates a tense silence. The facts of my circumstance bob, half-submerged, on it: I am here with Brad because he finally called me; I did not hate my childhood; I think a lot of gay people say that because they change significantly in their formative years; I have no one else to be around; at this moment, my ex is probably fucking my landlord. I consider that I probably look sad, and then that it might be the kind of sad Brad is bent on capturing in his photos.

"You look sad," he says.

"A beautiful kind of sad?" I ask. "I get that a lot."

"No, just like, tissues-sad."

I laugh and run a hand over the mermaid-cock, blurring the image. I redraw it. I am not a beautiful kind of sad, though I used to be, I think. I just realized it too late. There is a whole population of people, I know now, who have realized they were once attractive too late. Brad is not among them.

I speak to interrupt my own thoughts. "I mean, so this is your project. Which are you gonna do?"

"I'm thinking ocean," he says. I can sense him spreading out on the sand, relaxing. "I mean, have everything floating out, you know? Maybe at sunset. Nice light."

"And you're not going to collect it?"

"Nope."

"So you're going to take these photos and then, like, run away."

"I'm thinking some of the kids will keep some stuff, you know?" Something splashes out in the water, catching its food or being caught.

"Anyway, yeah. I mean, it's my project."

"It's also illegal, right?"

We sit for a while on the sand, which is cool to the touch. I cross my arms and imagine it makes me look defensive, so I smile slightly for no reason. When the mosquitoes come, we stand and walk to the shore. We can't see where we're going, which is part of the thrill, he tells me. We follow the sound of the calm surf lapping against the rocks. The moon is barely visible, a light curve in the sky. There is an element of romance that has attached itself like a leech to the night.

For a moment I think, I could just stay here. I could let him explain the shot—what its edges will be lost to, the significance of a sunset, or a sunrise. I could let him tell me what I already know: He's thinking of moving far away. He wants to be somewhere people say "y'all" and mean it. He missed me, and have I missed him?

The night is still, so unusually quiet I can hear the wind off the waves, the distant call of bells. My phone rests heavy in my sweatshirt. When we take that first step into the water, he says it's not that bad, and at first I think he's talking about his life.

TOUCH POOL

The heat of the leather steering wheel on his palms. The stillness of the night. The heaviness of his eyelids. The sudden flash of red lights feet ahead, the sharp turn of the wheel. The smell of burned rubber. The seat belt like a noose around his waist. The screech and thud of the car against the guardrail, then his weight thrown as his body caught up with the speed. The sudden crack of the windshield that he thought was his bones breaking. The push-pull of his shallow breath. The ghost of the deployed airbag in the passenger seat. The white smoke rising, the oval of steam around the rearview mirror. The fogged outline of his hand on the windshield. The torqued force of his heartbeat continuing as the car lurched off the road, crashing into the bushes, rolling under the palm trees and away from him, up into that sky lightening with morning. The far-off traffic light turning green. Nick's head against the wheel, while I placed mine against my pillow, wishing to never see him again.

———

"Come *on*," Nick said, and his hand slipped from mine.

Nick was leading me across the wide porch, through a group of shirtless men, their chests lightly shining with sweat. Music blared from somewhere below the hardwood, the bass vibrating in my sneakers. Inside the house, dim light flickered in the foyer. Nick and I were doing this "to prepare for college," where we had it in our minds people knew how to handle themselves in situations like these. Already I could sense the men around us figuring out we weren't invited. Nick had heard about the party from his only other gay friend, a guy named Micah who worked at a kind of upscale outlet mall across the street from our school. The night was shrouded gray with rising smoke from a bonfire out back. Nick breathed it in deep as we walked in, like he'd never smelled air so fresh. Someone behind me fell down the steps, so I turned around. Everyone surrounding the man laughed, and even Nick smiled. "God," he said, pulling me forward by the wrist, "even I can tell you've never been to one of these before."

"One of these" was referring to the gay Halloween party that we had invited ourselves to. That Nick had invited us to. He had driven us there, an hour outside Orlando, to a four-story home on the coast, the kind of home not normally populated by plastic red cups and dozens of men in togas and loincloths, lines of ash under their eyes. In T-shirts and shorts we were especially, embarrassingly clothed. But Nick was right; I had never been to one of these before. We made it through gold-lit hallways to the kitchen, which was empty, the counters reflecting a few spills. It occurred to me that didn't make sense, that that was where people should have been, but then I realized it was late, that we got there five hours after the thing had started, and everyone was on the porch, dancing, talking about their boyfriends, or their ex-boyfriends. They seemed like the kind of men to be lucky enough to have them.

"Whose *is* this?" Nick said, stopping at the green marble counter, piled with half-full bottles of rum and red wine. He wasn't asking anyone and didn't wait for a response. He lifted the Pinot, shrugged, and started to pour. I'd have called him out on stealing—something I've actually done before—but it seemed like the kind of place where "stealing" and "borrowing" could be easily confused, so I didn't. Nick squinted, a discerning look appraising the wine made instantly ridiculous by his T-shirt, which read, ALCATRAZ SWIM TEAM.

The screen door opened behind us, the wind reminding me how hot the house was, how few windows were open. A bald man in a Speedo walked past us, not even stopping to look.

"See, it's like I told you in the car," Nick said. He watched the man disappear upstairs, and finished his cup. He picked up the bottle and poured in the rest, offering it to me. "It's just what you wanted, Matt." He hopped up on the counter and sighed. "We're invisible."

———

Everyone knows Lia is going to be fired. A few months back, she accidentally broke the seahorse exhibit—knocked the glass with a feeding pole. Two weeks ago she killed twenty pounds of urchins after emptying an antiseptic into the kids' touch pool. She had mistaken the white tub of cleaner for a gallon of brine shrimp. We know it was twenty pounds because Sam, the shift supervisor, weighed them all in front of us on the scale used to chart the sea lions' growth. "Nineteen and a half pounds, folks," he said, trying to look all fifteen of us in the eye at once. He looked down to the urchins, piled in a purple pyramid on that metal block. "Slow clap for Lia, everyone."

AquaLand promises "a fun time for all," which is for the most part wrong, because, for the most part, we all hate it here. But it's hard to say, exactly—there's so much staff turnover. Lia, who's one of two senior biologists; Betsy, the gift shop girl; Ryan, who gives the demonstrations on how to feed the dolphins; and me—the guy who runs the stingray touch pool—we're the only ones who have been here longer than the span of a summer, the ones who have seen exhibits change and change back, the empty winter days and crowded summer nights: fireworks over the Octo-coaster, the lights clicking off—one by one—down the entry walk to the turnstiles.

But soon Lia is going to be fired. Sam will call her into his office, the walls lined with vintage posters of muscle cars. She probably won't cry as much as not understand.

She'll turn in her embroidered blue AquaLand smock and drive off into the Orlando traffic, up the searing hot turnpike, and disappear into the slanting saw grass, the bright sun off the shallow water in the Everglades, the small boarded house where she once lived with Lisa, the place she calls home.

It wouldn't bother me, her being fired. It wouldn't bother me under two conditions. If she weren't my aunt. And if she weren't dying.

The sound of boots hitting the pavement. The warm finger against his wrist. The gurney unfolding like a bear trap. The cool wind entering the car, the thickening ribbon of blood on his leg. The shards of fallen glass loosening and scattering onto the cement. The sun like a stoplight behind the glowing line of horizon.

When there wasn't any Pinot, he went looking through a cupboard. Nick is used to getting what he wants. For instance, he always gets the leads in the school musicals, is on the varsity diving team, and owns a dozen pet cockroaches despite his mother's hatred for insects, the traps she keeps for the same roaches Nick cares for in the basement boiler room. He has sharp, sculpted brows and makes bad puns in precalculus. ("Mathematical puns," he once said, "are the first sine of madness.") We met in sixth grade bio, became friends sitting at the front of the class. The nerds. Jump forward to senior year of high school, and we were still the same, mostly, except he turned into one of the theater nerds and I turned into one of the art nerds. A little more cleaning up, a little more shutting up, and he could have been the most popular guy in school. Of course—he didn't know it. So when another man walked in, opening the screen door and shaking sand off his feet, looking like the other from a few minutes ago, Nick had no problem talking to him.

"What's going *on* out there?" Nick nodded toward the porch.

The man looked at us, confused—maybe trying to figure out who we were. He crossed his arms. It occurred to me that he might be drunk.

"Dancing," he said, and furrowed his brow, as if the answer were obvious. Something glass and heavy shattered on the wood outside, and a high voice yelled, "That was Adam's, asshole!"

"That's it?" Nick asked. "Just dancing?"

"Some people are swimming," he responded.

We both paused. For a moment, Nick seemed vaguely confrontational, as if he needed to prove he was worthy of the conversation. He sat up on the counter, straightening his back. I detected a mean glint in his eye.

"I dive," Nick said. "On a team. We might go for a swim." It took me a moment to realize "we" included me, who hadn't actually swum since middle school gym.

The man looked to me. His nose appeared like a hawk's beak, slim and pointed, and cast a small shadow across his mouth. I could feel myself being noticed, judged, and looked away. The song outside changed, the starting pulse of "Material Girl," and a fresh wave of energy moved through the crowd. I tried to imagine what I'd do differently in college next year, how I would know when to get excited. When to ask about what's going on.

"I have to go to the bathroom," the man said, squinting his eyes, then leaving.

"So how's work?" Nick asked. "Everything good at the touch pool?" He peeled back the golden film on a bottle of cheap champagne he'd found above the fridge. My head was starting to warm, a pleasant push in my temples. I held out my cup for Nick to pour.

"It's okay, I guess," I said. "Some of the kids, though. They get so rough with the rays. One of them caught one by both flippers. He was trying to dance with it." I looked out the kitchen window. I could see the flaming eyes of tiki torches, hear the noise seeming to grow wildly and then calm to a muted lull—shouting followed by a sudden stillness that felt planned. I could sense Nick watching me, expecting more of a response. I got the sense I sometimes do that he wanted to finish up with me so that we could start on him. "It's just kind of like," I think aloud, "it grosses me out. All these kids have their hands in the tank. The rays don't have any say." The wine flushes my face. "It's like some metaphor."

"I guess. They do have a say, though," Nick said. He poked me on my arm, with one finger, like he was giving me a shot.

"What was that?" I asked.

"Stinger," he said, unwrapping a new bottle, pouring into a red cup. "Like this wine—so bitter. Think they have any mixers?"

"The rays don't *have* stingers. Lia de-barbs them," I said. I expected this to start conversation, but Nick was moving something in a lower cabinet.

"That guy, the second one," Nick said, "has such an *interesting* face. I think I might just *love* him."

Nick always made this joke about people he didn't like. He "just *loved*" them.

I could see myself blushing, even in the dark glass of the window. I didn't know what time it was, or even what we were going to do. The real problem was what I had actually until now hoped for, how we might have driven there together just to make something, anything, happen to us. But that was just one way of hiding the truth in a stranger's home, in dark Largo, on an October night stung with heat. I would follow Nick anywhere.

"And you're still doing those paintings, right?" Lia asks me.

She's cleaning out old tanks behind me, an assignment given to her by Sam, who probably has no use for them anymore and won't mind if they break. Several kids run up to the touch pool and lean against the faux rock. The rays glide along, black diamonds in the warm water, moving faster with excitement, waiting for someone to offer a hand across their backs.

I could try to play dumb with Lia, but it would feel insulting, so I say, "Yeah."

"Of the eyes?"

"Yeah," I say. "Eyes."

A boy slaps the water as a ray turns away. I walk over to

him, not just because one of the adults noticed, but because this annoys me. Even when people touch the rays, I want to tell them to stop—or when they pick favorites, when they try to *name* them. My job is a practice in not saying, *Leave them alone*, except for right now, when it gets to be.

"Leave that guy alone," I say. That's how it comes out— a kind of *no harm done* tone I can't seem to fix.

The boy looks up at me, wipes his hand on his jeans, and gazes back into the pool in a contemplative way that makes me think he's a liar and will grow up to be someone like Nick.

When I walk back to Lia, she's standing next to the tank, which is half-coated in a sheath of pink algae. This has happened a few times before, often at work. I wave a hand gently in front of her face, to no response. Her eyes are petrified straight ahead, but they're lifeless. Her shoulders are slouched forward, her body gone slack, the soft smoke of a recent cigarette around her. I take the yellow cloth from her loose hand and call for Betsy, who used to be an EMT. She runs over from the gift shop and sets a folding chair. I press my hand against Lia's lower back, in case she falls. I can feel her wavering in the air, a part of her detached and floating, like it might escape her. Betsy looks at the cloth in my hand and says, "Is that clean?"

"No," I say.

"Matt, I need a clean one. Now."

"Back room," I say. There's panic in my voice.

From behind me I hear a woman calmly say, "The man told you not to."

I look over my shoulder. The boy is clapping the water

again, a flurry of rays near him. His shirt is stained with water. "For fuck's sake," I loudly say, "leave them *alone*."

It's only after I say it I notice the crowd is thickening, people are curious, they're noticing Lia—and Sam is behind them. He's looking me right in the eye, a *Who do you think you are?* look on his face. Someone holds the boy's hands, and he starts crying. Lia's weight is more on my hand, she feels cold, her face paler, and Betsy returns with a wet cloth. The ambulance is fast.

Betsy says Lia will be okay, that it was just another episode, and tells me she needs to work sitting down. She says it like I'm not eighteen, like I'm old enough to care for someone else like this. Sam tells me he'll talk to me when things have settled. When I feel better, I put a damp cloth on my forehead too.

The climbing speed of the ambulance down the interstate. The flash of blue and red light against the emergency room entrance. The sliding doors closing like a drawn curtain.

The porch was colder than I remembered walking in, but my skin was numb, warming from the wine. Nick moved back among the men, needling his way through them with his shoulder, cup lifted overhead, but he wasn't leading me now. He wasn't urging me on, and I sensed that at any moment I could break away from him and it would take him a few minutes to even notice. It made me want to try.

But then his hand was on my wrist again, and at first I

felt grateful, relieved, before I noticed his palm was sweaty, and we were standing in a circle, and he was introducing me to people. I realized I didn't know what had happened at a certain point, that I had lost track of time. Micah was nowhere, and maybe hadn't even come at all. We were talking at the far edge of the porch to several men, who held each other around the waist and occasionally made meaningful eye contact. One of them said his great-great-grandfather invented dark chocolate.

Another claimed to pilot 747s, to have a discreet boyfriend whose "name you'd know."

"The water's still pretty hot," one of them said, looking off. "Freezing out here."

"I'm game," said Nick. It was the first time he'd spoken in a while, I realized, and he was drunk, gratingly eager to impress. He crossed his arms at his waist and took off his shirt, exposing a ripple of abs. He leaned against me, put his arm around my shoulders. I wondered if he was doing it to draw a comparison.

And then we were walking down those steps toward the water. Nick left his shirt on the ground, some kind of statement. His body was briefly illuminated as he passed by the light of a tiki torch. He was so thin I could see his ribs, even mistake them for muscle. He was ahead of everyone, and the group was laughing, and it seemed for a moment as if they were making fun of him.

The men spent several minutes wading in, getting comfortable, and I said I'd rest on the shore. I expected Nick to insist I go in, but he didn't—in fact, it was hard to tell where he was at all, the light hitting the water and confusing it, glimmering on its surface like a mirror. Sitting on the damp sand, next to a long snake of dried seaweed, I could sometimes make out a familiar face. The bald man with the sharp nose surfacing, Nick moving back into the group, which convened in a new circle every few minutes. Eventually, I heard voices coming closer behind me. Dozens of men were heading for the water. It embarrassed me that I was alone, so I stood and walked farther down the beach, my arms crossed. I felt suddenly angry at Nick for having left me, for having abandoned me so easily. I wondered if it had been his plan all along.

And as I was about to turn and walk away, back toward the house, to sit on that stool and drink whatever was left of that wine, I saw Nick's dark, thin body running out of the water, running at me. He was charging, and as he stumbled, I felt my stomach pitch. I realized instantly: The men were giving him shots out there—that was why they were circled, their heads arching quickly back. He was drunk.

"Matt!" he said. I could see the men looking in our direction, their attention focused on him. I moved back, and he stopped. "A shark!"

He was breathing hard, and what was attractive in him suddenly coagulated to a kind of pitiable, childish enthusiasm. I wanted to tell him to calm down, but that had never worked in the past, whenever he got a role he didn't want— passed up for a secondary part in favor of the lead—or when he didn't make the highest diving marks at meets. Those words—"Calm down"—only upset him. It occurred to me, standing there feeling the eyes of all those men on us, that Nick was actually *dangerously* competitive, that he

would win or die trying—which was something I knew
but that had never concerned me until then, where death
seemed to lurk in the water.

"Okay," I said, and held out my arm. I kept my voice
low and calm, hoping it might transfer to him. "Show me."

He took my hand with thoughtless force and led me up
the beach, over driftwood and mats of dried weed, our feet
pinched by broken shells, where he had apparently at one
point been, though I hadn't thought to look for him there.
My eyes adjusted to the dark, and I could see vague movement in the water—shadows of bodies moving and pulsing
with life. About a half mile up the beach, Nick squeezed
my hand and stopped, as if waiting to hear something. My
sweat made a small black heart on my shirt. He pointed
out and whispered loudly, "There."

I didn't see it at first, but then there it was, moving,
barely, on the sandbar. It was enormous, bigger than both
of us. It didn't make *sense* why it wasn't able to move. The
sandbar was shallow, but the creature was still partially
submerged, though it was hard to tell from so far away.
Nick started to walk out in the water a bit, and I felt myself
caught in the net of decision: to pull him back and risk
something between us, or to let him go and risk having
something awful happen to us.

"It's a spear," Nick said. "Something hurt it." He started
running out, in the water, the depth slowing him, pushing
with his arms.

"Stop," I said. I didn't realize I had started after him
until the warm water was at my knees, and then I had said,
without my own permission, "Nick, you're drunk."

He didn't hear me at first. He had dived under the water and come back up for air in a stupid show of rescue. I could read him too easily, tell too obviously how he wanted to say later he had saved something. But the closer I got, the easier it was to see the animal was already dying, that there was nothing either of us could do.

"Nick," I said again. "Stop. You're *drunk*."

He turned, the water rippling away around him. Without the sound of his splashing, I could hear loud laughter down the beach. It felt directed toward us both. The shark cracked its tail once against the water, a hard whip, closer than I expected.

"And I'm supposed to let it die?" Nick asked.

"It'll hurt you, Nick." I instantly regretted saying his name. I could hear it echo between us, condescending.

"Oh, so you're the expert."

"I've worked with sharks."

"You work," Nick said, "with *stingrays*." His voice was licked with contempt. "That don't even have stingers."

I had heard in school about how alcohol changed people, something I couldn't quite believe until now, witnessing that transformation firsthand. And like that, he was out of the water, past me. I couldn't tell what his plan was even as I tried to formulate my own, but I moved slowly toward the beach out of some instinct, trying to make my movement appear calculated, and reminded myself Nick would get back to the party without me eventually. Before Nick started to run up the dune, stumbling on the cooling and uneven sand, I could have sworn I saw a ray pass before me in the water, somehow darker than the water in the night.

How could I tell if the drink had changed me too? I didn't feel changed.

Sam calls me in after my shift, and I sit down in the only chair in his office, an old thing with wicker legs, upholstered, bursting seams.

"You don't need to sit," Sam says, looking through papers. I know Sam well enough to know he doesn't actually have that much work to do, and that he's trying to look busy. I stand, and he says, "But you can, if you want." So I sit back down.

Sam is a bad leader for these and other reasons, made powerful by his position managing this quarter of the park, the exhibits and keepers. He doesn't have much, but he has this, something I could sense from his micromanaging my interview a few years ago.

"What you said, to that kid earlier. Swearing? Inappropriate." He adjusts his glasses, small square frames. He looks tired, *sad* even, and it occurs to me he might be disappointed in me.

"I understand," I say, in case he is disappointed in me, not that I care.

"What do you want to do with your life?" he asks. The question feels too big for the conversation we're having. He pushes away the papers, trying to settle into a seriousness he can rarely summon without the help of some asshole comment.

"I want to paint."

"What do you want to paint?"

"I don't know," I said. My eyes lock on a porcelain shark near his computer, breaking with its triangular teeth a wooden sign that reads: SWIM AT YOUR OWN RISK, some kind of joke I don't get. He waits for a response, folding his hands. "I don't know," I say again. "Paintings."

I can tell he thinks I'm trying to make him seem dumb for asking the question at all, so I recover by confessing, "Eyes."

"Matt," he says. "Look. Why I called you in: We're closing the touch pool."

I feel a thump in my heart, then a lifting, but I don't pay attention to it. "Why?"

"It's just a liability, these things regrowing their barbs, you know—the major aquariums are doing it. Look." He slides a paper in front of me. It reads: *Permission for Release*.

"You're letting them go?"

"We're not putting them down."

"No, that's exactly what you're doing," I say. I can feel my face turning red. Someone knocks on Sam's door and he says, "Just a minute!"

"We just wanted you to know."

Lia opens the door, her brown hair unwashed. She's holding some of the promotional pamphlets we have for the new otter exhibit coming in. I want to ask her how things are, really, and whether she is okay, how Lisa was doing, if they had patched things up. I want to tell her to do something, to make some move, to go after what she wants. Instead, I look at my hands. I hear the screams from the Octocoaster outside, that excitement amplified like shot electricity in the air. I want to tell Lia I'm sorry. Even though I know I am only trying to tell myself.

The time in the seventh grade Nick pushed Aaron Sommers into the industrial fan at the winter dance for calling me a fag. The time Nick made me cut the tip of his finger with a scalpel to get him out of a bio midterm. The time we sat on a bench "sick" during baseball tryouts, and when the whole team was huddled on that field, the trees fluttering with hot wind upstage of that orange sunset, Nick asked me, "Should we kiss?" and I said, "That's okay." The time I shouldn't have said anything and closed my eyes and said yes.

"I was thinking about your thing, that thing you said," Nick yelled, walking up a dune. The sound of the party receded to a light static, and in its place was the gentle lapping of waves against the sand. In the distance I saw the men had lost interest in us—silhouetted dots moving in twos and threes back to the porch. "About people getting hands in our lives, how we need to tell them to stop—"

His inflection lifted, that's how I knew he wasn't done talking. He cocked his head up at the night sky, moonlight falling over the reeds bending in the wind, the tall grass, everything washed faintly gray. I put a hand on my hip and tried to look annoyed.

"I realized," he continued, "that's not the problem. That's not the problem at all." Screamed on the windy beach, from that far bump of sand, I realized how dumb my metaphor actually sounded. I had been feeling smarter, more together than him, and hated that he was right—it was just a dumb thing I said. "The problem," he said, his voice lowering with thought, "is how do we tell people to get their hands *in* our lives, right? That's the *real* thing."

I rolled my eyes and laughed. There was something absurd about extending the metaphor that far, I thought, spreading it that thin. They were rays in a tank. I didn't even know what I was talking about.

"It's just a *thing* I said," I said. "I didn't even mean it."

It occurred to me, even as I spoke the words, that I had meant them. I was trying to make him see reason, to get him involved, but I was doing it wrong—I knew I was doing it wrong—and it wasn't working.

"You know, Matt," he said. He raised his hands like he was caught in some act, taking a deep breath as if he were coming up for air. "I just *love* you."

Something in me frayed, then snapped. For just a moment, I wanted the upper hand back. I didn't know whether I meant it, but right then, I wanted to let him go.

"Keep it dramatic," I said, loud enough for him to hear.

I knew exactly how to hurt him. He turned and faced me, but he was too far away, backlit by the weak light from the party—I couldn't see what he meant by it. He nodded, finally understanding something, then turned and picked up toward the house, first at a jog, then running clear on the sand, arms pumping at his sides, until he was gone, his profile lost behind the thick brush, dark as the sky. And I was standing there alone. The breeze moved like a great thumb through the high grass. There was a distant clap of thunder, and the moonlight dimmed nearer to black. I felt proud and lost.

"Two kinds of places in this world," Lia says. She stands near the edge of the touch pool, looking out at the city, which is brought to a greasy black haze on the dimming horizon. A gray folding chair leans against the back of the touch pool. She got off her shift an hour ago but hasn't taken off her smock, and I wonder if she's trying to make a point. "Places you like and places you'd like to set on fire. And then there's this."

She laughs a little as she says it, gesturing out with a cigarette in one hand, the other resting over her stomach.

I know she's telling me something she's heard before, or maybe saying something she talked about with Lisa. And I sense I'm not old enough for the conversation she wants to have, and that she knows it. Behind me, the rays move over shrimp I just emptied into the touch pool, their wings splashing the water. A siren sounds down the freeway, coming toward us. Lia checks her watch. We live together in this moment, separate from each other. She exhales, the smoke curling up like a wish around her. I close my eyes and breathe it in.

I felt proud and lost. I know now which feeling lasts.

CLEARWATER

I tell the policeman I didn't touch the rib cage. This isn't entirely true. I was walking the Florida sandbar, observing a floral pink stripe of sunset on the horizon, thinking (okay, selfishly) of what would happen to me once Jeffrey passed, when I tripped over the bones. Disturbed, they leaned and relaxed with the incoming tide, the gait of a rocking chair.

"Where's it?" the man asks me. He's young, red weals pocking his face beneath the recent stubble of a shave. His badge reads: *Clearwater PD*. Gray birds wheel overhead, having spotted an easy kill in the parking lot.

I point toward its location, near a lone buoy. Two teen girls volley a rainbow beach ball feet away from where I suspect the bones rest. He whistles sharply, calls them in. They chase each other out of the water, laughing, an imagined shark at their heels.

"You sure it was a person's?" I can tell he doesn't think I'm sure.

"I think so," I say.

Hours ago, another horror: Jeffrey's chest glowing, para-normal, up on that screen in the hospital, a phosphorescent blossom on the right side. The doctor then held up an identical photo, a smaller bud of white, a poisonous flower yet to bloom: "And this was two weeks ago," he said with a sigh. Later, I told Jeffrey no one was to blame as he finished a cup of shivering red Jell-O. A lie we might as well believe.

"So you're not sure," he says. His radio clicks with static. "Divers are on their way."

He retires to his idling car, and I walk toward the shore-line. That he's let me wander assuages my fear I might be suspect in some unknown murder, one of those killers hopelessly entwined with their victims. I remain on the beach partly out of a sense of obligation for having located the bones, but also because I want to see them found, lifted, bagged, gone.

Sitting on the sand, it occurs to me for the first time that beneath the waves there may be other parts: elbows, fe-murs, submerged spines and patellae. They have to be out there, somewhere. On other beaches, in other countries, rolling up in warm, shallow water, caught in the wire of fish traps set deep out in bays. Every day things like this must turn up, though we can't recognize them. I make an impression with my palm in the sand. When I lift my hand, its shape is quickly lost to the wind.

TOURNIQUET

I used to think a tourniquet was a kind of flower. I was sure I'd heard my mother say she planted rows of them when I was younger: bulbous yellow things, unburdened by petals, slick with dew, shining like sugar in the frost of a March fog. It wasn't until I'd gone to nursing school in my mid-twenties, one of those fresh starts, that I learned a tourniquet is a compression tool, a vise for flesh, a thing that says, *I am holding you together*. I don't remember which flowers I'd mismatched, improperly bouqueted out of their meanings. Years later, on the drive home from a shift cleaning knife wounds and wrapping burnt hands in gauze, I'd stop at a farmers market, poring over flowers, remembering. "Azalea," a woman told her daughter, pointing to a red-pink haze. "Chrysanthemum."

IN THE PALM OF HIS HAND

The first thing I have to confess is that pretending to have a relationship with the church (The Church?) came easily to me, in a way that at the time did not feel like a sin.

"A relationship with God, you mean. You're not praying to a building."

My friend Maggie had been out of Fordham for four months and found, back in her Vermont hometown, a need to reaffirm, at every turn, her hundred thousand dollars of intelligence and acquired wisdom. The phone crackled with static, her bad reception up there in the woods. I imagined her in the middle of a brown leaf pile, neck high, and stifled a laugh at the image. She continued disapprovingly, "It's worth asking: Is this *ethical*?"

"You mean moral," I said.

"No," she said, aghast with the special irritation at having been corrected by someone who graduated from a state school. "I mean *ethical*."

"I guess I'm not worried about that," I said. She didn't reply immediately. I could tell I was upsetting her more but pressed anyway. "Didn't you do kind of the same thing? Saying you played tennis for Bryan?"

"That actually could have been true. I have the body for it. Plus, I can pick that up anytime."

"And I can't just start going to church?"

"Again," she insisted, "it's about going to *God*. And for your first relationship?"

"Plenty of people who go to church don't believe in God."

"Ugh," she said. "You sound like Bill."

Bill was a contrarian who Maggie had dated and complained about through her sophomore year, a Columbia guy with long black hair he modeled on weekends who pushed back on everything she said, and who once infuriatingly "iced" her on a fire escape during a party. A shame memory for us both. She'd called me right after, and I'd been too drunk myself to be of any help. She still hadn't gotten over him, I knew, and I felt awful that she still couldn't see a fact so clearly before us both, obvious even at the time: Bill never really liked her. She was trying to become him now, though I'd never tell her that. *You sound like Bill*, I wanted to fire back.

"Sorry," I conceded instead. Throwing the conversation in the trash, I said pointlessly, "What are your plans for the day?"

She ignored the question, the phone making a crinkling, fading-out noise that suggested the fraying of our friendship with each of these less and less frequent calls.

"Why are you even doing this? Is a guy worth *all this energy*?" She strung up those words, put extra spaces between them for emphasis: All. This. Energy.

It was something I would have said to *her*, might already even have. I had the urge to get off the phone, which seemed to come at me from out of the blue but in truth had been lurking all along. I touched my chest where I imagined the metal Jesus resting, proving my devotion.

"Maggie, you just have to understand. He's like—he's so, so hot. He has one of those fucking butt chins."

"So you said you were Catholic?"

"*Christian*," I corrected, not totally sure of the difference. "Leaves me options, right?"

"Is this worth eternal damnation?" she said. I laughed.

We were two different people now, and scheduling the conversation felt like a display of my loneliness, a feeling the city often made me think I might finally be getting rid of. The past few months, I had started to know that Maggie hated that we had switched places, and now it was my turn in the city, and despite what we'd both believed would happen, I was the one making it. And in fashion. It felt like a gift that I had to succeed at all costs. Not because I wanted to pull for a September issue or boss around an assistant, but because it created distance between who people thought I used to be; it *made* them know they were wrong.

"Probably I'm already damned," I said. "Is avoiding that even an option for me at this point?"

Eric and Amy moved their chairs up to my desk, rolling them noisily along the long corridor of glass conference rooms, revealing to anyone within earshot their status as forever-assistants, unpromotable people who never get why they're not promoted. They were the kind of people I risked letting myself become when I indulged their gossip and exclusive group lunches. Their unprofessionalism was contagious in that it gave the impression I was like them, which I wasn't. *Charm Magazine* handed out one promotion every two years, on the same date—the next day. People called it the day someone gets Charmed. New though I was, six months in I'd heard during a performance review that I was being eyed for it. A secret I'd kept at all costs.

"So the date," they said. "The church guy."

"His name is Simon!" I said.

"He's so hot," Eric said. "Like, *dreamy*. I went on a date with a guy like this once. He ordered sushi. I could barely speak."

Amy and I stared at him. The sushi detail read as pathetic.

"How are you playing this?" Amy said. She rolled her chair up closer. "You need a game plan."

"I should get a cross," I joked.

Eric gasped loudly. "My God, that's genius." In her office his boss, one of the top fashion editors, leaned back in her chair, wondering what had caused it.

"Probably worth a shot actually," Amy said.

"I don't know if I'll see him again."

"I have to pull for the deciduous shoot this afternoon. I'll see if we have a prop or something."

The "deciduous leaves shoot" was Eric's promise at a good idea that every one of us knew would get killed last minute, and we were thankful for it. He'd saved up all his trust for this moment. The gift of self-elimination.

"Eric," I said, "if I do it I'm getting a real cross."

He nodded and I told them I needed to get back to calendaring lunches. Overkill? Maybe. It seemed worth it, to have this insane attention to detail. As they screeched their chairs down the hall, I wanted to tell them how I'm succeeding and why they're not: that I come in on Sunday nights to do memos. Call down to the front desk to have the nineteenth floor lights turned on. I leave with strain in my lower back from hunching over my keyboard for hours. I shut myself up pretty much all the time. I wanted to just finally say, *Stop talking to me. You aren't getting Charmed; I am.*

My roommate, Dave, was a gaymer on weekends and, during the depressive episodes that were becoming a regular feature in his life, every other day of the week too. He'd quit two good jobs and been left unable to find another.

When I got home from work, he was talking into an earpiece with several other men like him, gays who don't moisturize and spend their money on consoles not condoms. He met them all on some online forum I had been avoiding asking about, and I resisted the urge to pity him because he was such a nice guy. Even asking him to help clean the shower left me doused with guilt.

"Hey," I said. "How's the day?"

He took off his headset fast. "Hey! Okay. How are you?"

"Wiped," I said. "Long day." I didn't mean to upset him, but bringing up that I had a salary touched a nerve, I could tell, so I kept on. "How's the game?"

"Oh, it's good! Yeah, good."

"What's the point?"

"Kill the bad guys," he said, laughing a little. "As always."

"Who are the bad guys?" I dropped my brown leather satchel near the couch and walked toward the screen.

"This one is pretty messed up. You go to different areas and, like, take whole places out. They're filled with bad guys though. But weird I guess."

"Almost makes you seem like the bad guy, huh?" I said.

"Yeah," he said. He was choking through his words a bit, flustered. "But I'm not."

I normally never got this close to Dave. He had an aura of palpable sadness, covered up with desperation. I could always see it from a distance, but getting too close left me unable to exit conversations gracefully. I always had to shut him down, and every time I did, I knew it just made things worse. He had paid his rent on time these past few months, with life-or-death deadline urgency. Last month he told me, his forehead shining with anxious sweat, leaning nervously on my bedroom doorframe, that he'd be a little late. He'd been close to tears. I couldn't help but think if I were him I'd have just secretly sent my check in late, that it really didn't matter. Later on, he'd shown up in that doorframe again and asked if I wanted to get a beer. The first time we'd have hung out. I told him I had plans, and then quickly made them, as if to prove to myself I could do such a thing. An hour later, I was laughing at a bar down the street with Ashley and Lauren, hoppy foam on my upper lip.

I sat down next to him on the couch and saw the thin gold chain around his neck. "I like that," I said.

"Oh!" He took it out, the chain hung slack. "My mom gave it to me. She said I should always wear it."

"It looks good on you," I said, offering him a kindness I didn't mean.

"Thanks! I have others if you want this one."

"Really? Or I could have one of the others," I said. *Are you this entitled?* I thought, just to myself. *Taking your roommate's cross?*

"Yeah, it's totally fine!" He struggled it around his head and cupped it in the palm of his hand, holding it out for me. "She sends them to me a lot." I took the cross from him. There was a greasy quality to the metal. He grabbed at his headpiece fast, noticing something blinking on the screen.

"Sorry," he said. "We've been waiting on this battle. We finally got access to the vampire armory."

"No problem," I said, hoping the secondhand embarrassment at his lameness wasn't obvious in those words. And then I went off to wash the cross in the kitchen sink.

I lifted my head from his pillow, sitting upright on Simon's couch, and adjusted my shirt (as planned) to the side so that the thin gold chain that led down to a crucifix, carved out with a tiny Jesus, flashed against my neck.

"Oh," Simon said. "Did you have that last time?"

Glad as I was Simon had noticed, I expected for the noticing to go something like this: a quiet acknowledgment I was religious too. Eventually, a new intimacy deepened by the respect of this choice, which would (also eventually) lead through a few small devotion-proving fights to love and then marriage. I had not expected to have to confront my religiousness aloud just yet, and for a moment the lie seized me around the waist. "Yeah," I told Simon, measuring my voice, trying to make the word sound aggressively mundane, as if I spoke of the chain often. "I wear it everywhere."

I had worn it only once, to the grocery store the day before, in a dumb practice round of trying to pull "the look" off in public after he'd texted to ask what I was up to the next night. *What is the look?* I wondered to myself. *Do I walk differently now? Does this make people think I'm not gay? That I'm not comfortable with my gayness?* My internal dialogue was running at such a high level that I had forgotten half of what I'd gone to the store to get—chicken and rice, a roll of toilet paper Dave hadn't bothered to buy despite the recent assurances of his accountability. ("I know it annoys you—sorry, I'll get it tomorrow!")

"That's really cool," Simon said, placing a glass of water in front of him. What would have been a normal gesture of hospitality felt oddly like a profession of love. *Really cool.* Not just cool. It pleased me; this was working.

"Thanks," I said, injecting a hint of weariness into the word. "A lot of people don't understand it." I adjusted my shirt so the chain disappeared, and we got back to talking about the movie we were about to watch, a Christian horror film called *Bells of Reckoning* in which nuns become vampires and then turn absurdly and confusingly back into nuns.

"Have you seen this one?" Simon asked.

"I haven't!" I said. *Obviously*, I thought to myself. The movie case looked like a bargain-bin novel, fanged nuns in idiot red tones. I was comforted by the fact we had ended the moment on a note of my honesty (no, I had not in fact seen this movie), and placed my head at an angle, so that if Simon wanted to, he could nudge me to fall romantically onto his lap. The only scene that held my attention was the one where the nuns become unpossessed, their fangs shrinking back to human teeth. It reminded me of the cool crucifix above my heart, and what it would mean for me to break through the illusion of my Catholicism, which was amazingly simple to pull off.

"Church Sunday?" he asked.

"Of course," I said. Of course.

Maggie called me at exactly five thirty the next day, a punctuality that seemed desperate. "I have him wrapped around the palm of my hand," I told her excitedly right when I picked up, walking to the subway. I wanted her to say anything that would support this decision, this certainty that we can change for other people, or ourselves. Maybe private school taught that.

"Isn't the expression '*in* the palm of your hand'?"

"Both!" I said.

"It can't be both. That doesn't make sense."

"How's Bryan?"

"Rough patch but every rough patch ends."

"Yeah, I hope so too," I said.

"You hope what?"

"That every rough patch ends."

"I didn't say I hope. I said it does."

"Sorry," I said, letting her win.

In the background, over the bustle of cars and distant horns, I heard, "Mag, where the fuck you put the tomatoes?" I winced at how embarrassed it must have made her feel, knowing I heard that.

"I have to go," she said. "Did you get the cross?"

"I'm wearing it now," I said. "I actually like it."

She sighed loudly, sparing me the sense this was about me at all.

"I have to go too," I said. "Dinner with friends in the Village."

She didn't tell me what she was going to do, so I was sure it was nothing she wanted me to know. I walked down into the subway and waited ten minutes for a train and didn't think of her once. I imagined myself going through *Charm*'s closet with Eric in the next few days, pulling out church-wear. *White and black*, I told myself. But I honestly had no idea.

"You deserve it. I've always known it'd be you," I told Eric outside, waiting for him to finish his cigarette. Steam pummeled angrily up from a vent down the street. Eric had just gotten tapped to be Charmed that morning, and I was caging in my fury. His boss had walked over to him with a cake heavy with vanilla frosting that read in florid red cursive: *You're a Charmer!* The whole spectacle of the promotion felt too rich, condescending in a way that made me question whether I really even wanted this anymore. I had thought the crowning would be a little quieter. For the first time I wondered if I might be too good for the job; the idea I had given up too much for it upset me.

He made a face, like he was about to cry. "That means a lot. Thanks. I honestly thought it might be you." He laughed.

"Oh please!" I smiled knowingly, performing for him how ridiculous that must sound to me. "No, not my time."

But it was my time, and I knew it. A taxi pulled over in front of us, two young women stepping out, bright yellow high heels.

"Fuck, my three o'clock," he said.

"Them?"

He didn't answer. He stabbed out his cigarette and walked quickly back into the lobby with a new kind of confidence I seethed at. His refusal to finish the conversation felt like a personal attack. *That's my three o'clock*, I thought, just to myself. You just sat your ass down and never got up.

Dave could tell I was pissed when I walked in the door. He turned off the game right away, and I saw his face in the blank screen ahead of him, tired. I almost asked him if he'd even gotten any sleep.

"What's got you grumpy?" he asked.

"I'm no Charmer, not today." He seemed not to remember I had told him about this, about work, or maybe I had never told him. Either way, I felt myself blame him.

"Still wearing that cross though! I like it!"

He smiled his big, fake grin, and I wanted to tell him to take a shower.

We arrived at the church five minutes before the Mass started. The air outside was thick with the syrupy scent of frankincense or something like it. Whatever it was exactly, the smell was just left of Christmas at my rich aunt's. Simon's dirty blond hair, parted, slicked down, started to get me hard, so I bit my tongue. The crucifix felt invisible, the temperature of my chest, as if it had melted right into me.

Outside the large stone entrance, people were folding their hands, bowing their heads. Small groups formed, the ominous groan of an organ warming up its hundred throats. When we walked inside, Simon dipped his fingers in a bowl of water and made a cross. I could see him touch, left-right, across his chest, and did the same. A small drop of water lingered at the corner of my brow, and I sensed that at any moment it might bore a hole right into my head, announce me as the impostor I was. We sat on the end of the hard pew in the back. What kind of choreography did one do in the church? Whose lead did I follow? Suddenly, I felt more at risk of being exposed than ever before. What was the padded green bar under the pew ahead of us *for*? How long did this even *last*? Growing up, I'd heard friends talk about how Mass dragged on. Were we talking hours?

We rose at the sight of the pope. The pope? Was that a

priest? It was *not* a shaman. The pope was the one in charge. *Ah*, I thought. *Vatican.*

He greeted us warmly; we stood, then we took our seats. I thought, *Game time.* One eye always on Simon. I stood behind him, sat after his lead, a power play unknown to him that registered in me as sexy. At several points we sang, "Hosanna in the highest!" And I found the tune kind of catchy. After what seemed like an hour (it had been an hour), there was a scene playing out about the Body and Blood of Christ, and I realized I was going to have to commit. To eat the Body of Christ.

Simon's shoe lifted the bar we'd been kneeling on, and he gave me a look. Like pride. Guilt surged through me. We attached ourselves to the back of a long line of everyone. (Nothing I could have sat out.) We moved forward with a kind of overly mindful step-touch. It made everyone look pretty gay.

A few people ahead of me eyed what looked like crackers as the priest lifted them, mumbled a thing, and then placed them in the palms of hands.

I heard Maggie's voice, singsong, almost funny: *Eternal damnation.*

I saw people bypassing the goblet so (unlike me) skipped on the wine. When we got to the back, Simon took my hand. I almost gasped. He led me to the foyer, where a few hymnals were scattered on the floor, that water I dabbed myself with on the way in—and he kissed me. I could still taste the grape juice. *The Blood of Christ*, I almost said aloud, just to correct myself.

———

A few days later, Amy stopped by my desk, looking around suspiciously. It was the kind of care I didn't expect from her, and both this and the attention she'd paid to her red-brown hair, which waterfalled down onto her shoulder, gave me a jump of sit-up respect I normally didn't experience with her.

"So, about Eric," she said. "What do you think?"

Amy was a famous gossip, so I never got to know her. ("*Smart*," a photo assistant Lexi had said during drinks one day, revealing some experience she didn't want to share. "Very smart.")

"I don't know," I said, tired of being in a dishonest mode. "I'm happy for him."

"Yeah," she said, leaning against my desk. "He's been here four years."

"Four years?" I said. "That's insane."

"Yeah, it is. He tells all the new hires he's coming up on two." She ate some peanuts I didn't know she had in her hand. "Kind of embarrassing."

I felt a reminder not to disclose anything about myself. "Good for him," I said again, trying to pump the words full of meaning, trying to mean them.

She sighed. "They told you you were up for it, didn't they?"

"What do you mean?" I said, feeling a heavy thud in my heart.

"Oh, they do that with everyone. Makes you work hard like crazy," she said.

"They told you?"

"They still tell me."

"Why are you telling me this?" I said.

"Honestly? So you can take yourself out of the game," she said. "Four years? Four *years*," she said, making a face like she'd just witnessed a grimace-worthy football play.

"Have you really been here for just two years?" I asked her. I hoped my ability to see through her shit would override my anxiety at having bought into all this crap. Crap on crap on crap.

"Three," she said. "And a half." She paused for a moment. "So I'm next. By the way, I like the chain on you," she said. "It's a good look. You need the edge."

I took it out from under my shirt, feeling the bumps of the little Jesus in my fingers. "It feels bad," I said. "To be honest. To wear this and not mean it."

"You really can't have that much of a conscience," she said. "Obviously he likes you."

"Anyway, I don't care about getting Charmed," I said, trying to end the conversation. Just after I said it my eyes darted around, making sure no one that mattered had heard. The lie felt strong, bulletproof, but my eyes were starting to water, so I didn't look at her. Amy laughed. She clapped her hands free of the peanut residue and placed one on my desk, staring into me. "Yeah. I said that too."

My key didn't open the lock. The knob felt stuck. I fumbled with it, then knocked on the door. "Dave?" I eyed the keyhole. "Dave? Can you open this up, please?"

I knew he was home. I heard gunshots on the television screen. "Dave, can you open this?" I yelled louder. Sometimes the headpiece was hard for him to hear through.

Finally, the lock gave. On the screen, Dave was out—no lives left. Blood punched at the monitor, paintballs of it. I put my bullshit keys on the bar cart and felt a lifting in me for some reason, like finally I wanted to just talk to him. It looked like they'd beaten the armory and were on to someplace else. It almost looked like a church.

I froze when I turned the corner into the hallway, my body shivering up, standing reflexively on tiptoe, like a ghost at the sight: blood traveling in a thin chain, slow, down a divot in the hardwood, from the bathroom. It looked like grape juice.

I stopped in my tracks and called Maggie instantly. My hand shook, and my voice erupted with panic, everything I couldn't keep in bursting out. She was in a good mood when she answered.

"What's got you grumpy?" she said.

"I think my roommate killed himself."

"You know," she said, laughing a little, "you don't always need to be dramatic."

"He's in the bathtub, I think." The silence between us fell, hard, to the floor.

"I'm going to call someone."

"Can you just stay on, for just a second? Dave!" I called again. I didn't want to face it. I had nothing to feel sorry about, not a thing in the world. Maybe no one else did either. Behind me, gunshots. A tiny, triumphant voice through his headset: "Got him!"

Since I was a child, watching my older brother play video games, I had the idea that when we die we are taken to something like an end screen to give away our goodness and our badness, the sum accumulation of all we've done, before our game really ends. I want to give Dave everything. All of it. Not because I care, but because I can't keep it for myself. I looked at what the truth was doing to me, disgusted, and wondered if he's giving it all to me right now, before that red light on his console turns off.

Date four was Simon's plan to help me heal. He said that certain views can mend a heart, God calling out clear over the hills, after I phoned him crying. Through the insanity of that moment, my tears slicking that glass, I recalled feeling perversely happy that an awful thing was bringing us closer together, and it made me wish for the suffering I had.

So it's right now, right now. Simon and I have made it to the top of that abandoned fire tower upstate where God had visited him two years ago in a breath, something he told me on the drive there. God told him he could be gay, but he had to be careful. Date the right guy. We drove through piles of fall leaves kicking up past us, like the deciduous shoot that had actually turned out well. Not that I was there to see it with my paid leave.

On the walk up, I admired the way he moved, sometimes taking two of those rickety metal steps at a time, an eagerness for the view that seemed too pure for me. Looking out now over the trees, the sunset, all that glimmering beauty, an apology rises in me. I don't even know who it's for, but I don't want it for myself. For the first time, I know Simon wants to kiss me. He thinks I'm finally safe to love. I've passed all the tests. A hot breeze hits us, and I watch its path through the trees, fluttering their orange-brown leaves like a spirit. Will he still love me when I tell him the truth? Will he still love me if I tell him the truth? *The faith is in me*, I want to say. *I promise it is. I just don't think it's where you want it to be.*

Picture perfect, I'm wearing almost everything I've borrowed from *Charm*'s closet, throwing around orange patterned shorts and spiky overthought shoes with Eric that day when we knew this is where we'd be, back when I thought I could have a clear conscience about all of this, like it wasn't just going to hurt me in the end. The brown belt that risks, but fashionably. My white sleeves cut up higher than a short sleeve, highlighting the place my bicep starts. Suddenly, I wonder if I just look ridiculous, someone trying so hard for something they don't need, or can't sustain. That anxiety gives birth to a fact I know I wear well: I just look stupid.

Simon turns to me and says, "Let's pray."

"Okay," I say.

He has one of his serious moments, looking up with those gorgeous eyes, like a *Charm* cover model. "I'm so glad we met," he says.

"Me too," I say. I fold my hands on the cold metal bar. When I close my eyes, I wonder if maybe he's in a tower taller than this one, looking down on me. But I don't believe it, not for a second. *I love you, Dave*, I think, and try to make myself feel it. That cool metal cross just over my heart, the one I won't ever take off. Entering this prayer I can't leave. A breeze coming now from the other direction, moving my hair back into place—picture perfect. Simon with his proud smile. No clue of those words but the first two. *Dear God,*

DOUBLE EDGE

The cold blade lodged in my throat like it always did, the glare of the spotlight hot on my face. What I had to do was hold the sword for a few moments, my tongue pressed against the base of my mouth, and exhale as I lifted it out, its edge sliding against my throat, between my front teeth. Afterward, I was meant to quickly bow and move ringside so the stallions could rear wildly, followed by the standing elephants, then our impatient ringmaster, whose whip cracked the air in yellow sparks. It wasn't hard to know what went wrong. I tasted my saliva souring, and as the drums crescendoed into a rush and a piercing stillness took the tent, the blade turned, catching on my molar and digging into my gum. In the version of the story I planned to tell Miles, I would blame my sweating palm, the widening of my throat with a gagging cough. I wouldn't tell Miles it happened just as I decided to look for him in the stands—the shock of his graying hair, a bright polo pulled tight with muscle—and realized he hadn't come.

The neighing of the horses as they were held back. My

careful lean onto the padded orange gurney, the doctor whose job it was to gently hold the metal hilt, which winked with light as I passed beneath the entrance marquee. My eyes glazing with warm tears. The sudden cold of the night, the reminders to breathe. The distant chirring of crickets. The vibration of the metal in my throat with the revving ambulance, nurses with hands over their mouths in the ER.

I didn't know until a few days later, after I was discharged, that Miles had given me no reason. When I called him, he didn't pick up. I drove to his house late one night, half a bottle of merlot swirling in my gut, and saw his shadow in the window, but when he noticed my car outside he turned his lights out. I opened the car door and listened to the hot wind move through the willow trees but couldn't bring myself to do anything else. I swallowed so hard it felt as if that blade were back in my throat, pitching it open.

Before Miles there had been Chuck, and before Chuck, Charlie, a venture capitalist with blackout curtains drawn on every window in his apartment. "For insomnia," he'd told me.

I had met him outside of a show and days later at a bar and been transfixed by his desire to bring up, at almost every chance, the fact his wife would classify our date as cheating. I did not find it sexy exactly, but I could not understand his obsession with me until hours later when, drunk and alone with him in his apartment, he gestured to PVC pipe leaning against the wall near the shoes. He explained that, seeing me, he'd been "impressed." Then it made sense that he had watched my throat as I drank that martini, his interested pupils moving slightly with the lift of my Adam's apple as I swallowed. I closed my eyes and kneeled at his feet. As he sunk the plastic into me, I sensed a danger that felt like desire until his fingers touched my lips and he gently pushed my head back, the pipe moving past where the metal had ever gone.

When I met Miles he looked me in the eye. He noticed the way I got upset. It was strange to love someone first for their ambivalence, but it was how the love had started, and I assumed later, waiting for him in my car parked outside his dark home, how it had ended.

It would take me a few years to return to performing, though I'd practice raising the sword in my kitchen and bedroom during nights when I couldn't sleep, its blade catching moonlight through the windows. Things would be different. I would be more careful, hold the sword every time as if it really could kill me if only I blinked the wrong way. And when the spot rose again from the worn dirt of the ring and onto my face, its heat on the bridge of my nose, I wouldn't be looking for Miles. I would try to feel the applause when I bowed. I would stand outside the tent after shows talking to families, promising that the sword is real. I would wait a few years and throw the old sword away, but before I would I'd look for any indication of the accident—a scratch, a film of dried mucus. But there would be nothing; I would be able to see my whole face in that blade.

At some point during my time away, the show added

another act. I see it each night now, from under the stands, between the legs of families. It's called the Vanishing, placed just before the bows. Two clowns, some new hires, stand against a white wall that's rolled to the center of the ring. They each strike a pose against it, as if blown back by a great wind, and hold hands. There is a piercing flash of light—the whole tent briefly consumed with a golden mist. The orchestra gets loud and brassy. And when sight returns, applause takes the tent in a fever. Both have become silhouettes, shadows.

Tonight, I ask the ringmaster if I can sit in the audience to see it. It's one of our last runs of the season. He says okay, that I owe him. I nod and walk around to the back. Several rows are empty, and I sit near the exit. The air smells of cotton candy and rust. I wonder what I look like in the ring from this distance. I wonder if there's ever a way to see myself like that—really.

When the time comes for the Vanishing, I make a point to watch for what happens to the clowns, but the light is too bright. I blink, and I miss it.

After the show, I find one of the contortionists at his spot outside the tent. He doesn't look like he wants to talk—he's stretching out a knot in his leg—but I ask him anyway. "Where do they go?"

"Hell," he says, plucking the cigarette from his mouth. "Even I don't know."

MOORING

It's a true story because it's a story I tell you. But you want the story with the facts, the stuff we both know. Everything that happened—so here it is.

I had the nagging suspicion I'd chosen the wrong cabin from the moment we both arrived, parking just before dusk at the fork down the long gravel driveway. Inside, the larger things checked out: deer antlers mounted on a far wall, curving up in two thorny parentheses. A small blue vase on the dining room table, likely my mother's, that had gathered dust. "Finn always loved these," I said so Luke might overhear, picking up an old book of crosswords, mostly unfinished. I was waiting for Luke to ask what, but he was too far away. The crosswords felt like a gross metaphor, but my father really might have loved them. It might have been true.

Okay, fine, I told myself. I'm a liar—I lie. I was in my

father's cabin and had told Luke it was Finn's. You do what you need to, to save what you need. To close one story and open a chance for the truth.

Luke walked around the house, doubling back while looking at the ceiling for some way up to the roof. I was surprised to hear the slide of collapsible stairs and raised my voice to ask how he'd found them. "Believe it or not, I grew up in a place just like this!" His footsteps shook the metal beams and thudded onto the roof.

I felt a paranoid jump in my heart, remembering a scene from months back: From my cheap seats on the balcony, I saw Luke below in the crowded orchestra, waiting for a show to start. I looked for who had gone with him, who he had taken instead of me. When the light onstage cast even a momentary glow back onto the audience, I tried to see his shadow in the darkness. I missed most of the production, constantly waiting to see, to have my paranoia justified, but never learned for certain if he'd really taken anyone. I started having two distinct nightmares, both about that moment, in which he was either gone or right next to me, smiling, a warm hand on my thigh. These were my options—romance or death. Sometimes I added another element to that pain, imagining Finn as the person next to him, the lines of my stories blurring away.

Pushing my father/Finn's tattered curtains aside, gazing out at the thick forest of pines he had planted before I was born, I did not see any light from the neighboring cabin between those branches. The Realtor had mentioned the place was "on the right, you'll see," but it wasn't until after I had arrived and opened the car door to that syrupy air, after we walked into the mudroom that smelled like wet dog, the place unlocked as I'd been told it would be, no numbers or mailboxes, just tall weeds, overgrown—that I considered I had misunderstood. Out the window, the trees swayed ominously in the dusk. I entered the whole scene of the cabin as an actor might, waiting for his chance to dart off into the wings, for the curtain to close.

The kitchen, the marble sink, the bathroom—did not feel familiar exactly, but I had prepared myself not to recognize much. It also felt oddly lived in, though of course my Finn had passed only a few days before.

Twenty-two years he had lived here. My father. Finn— how long? Five, I decided, in case I needed that knowledge later. I leaned against the marble counter, considering, just to myself. Why did I get the place? Four siblings, all of whom were alive, all of whom were on better terms with my father than I was. The only explanation I could think of is that the place was a kind of gift, the result of all that sorrow bubbling up last minute. (My sister had agreed: "Kind of a shit little place," she'd said. "I keep forgetting you haven't been.") She resented that I had been chosen to inherit it, I could tell; every few months we spoke, she'd laughed about her plans for the land, a quaint summer getaway with her husband. She mentioned a bulldozer once, in a way that felt violating, like retribution for something she'd never told me. I imagined lines struck through in my father's will with a shaking hand, my name written in.

Footsteps thudded overhead, Luke making his way back to the hatch, and rain began to strike the glass. Little scars, one after the next.

"Babe," Luke said. "You didn't tell me you invited anyone."

"What?" Instantly, I imagined creating a friend for Finn, then anxiously swatted the idea away.

"Are they bringing food?" Luke added. "That fridge is weird."

"Who?" I walked to the fridge. A fresh wave of nausea roiled inside me. Six cases of beer, stacked. Half a discount apple pie. And milk, with a far-off enough expiration date to confirm my fear in a flash: We were in the wrong house.

"That pie is fine," Luke said, defeated. "I guess."

A beam of light moved across a far wall, shadows stretching like something out of a horror movie, contorting silhouettes. Headlights. The rain coming down harder, sky burning with the first rumbles of thunder.

"Oh, for fuck's sake," I said, taking Luke's hand.

"I'm sorry!" Luke said. "The apple is fine, really!"

I took my wallet and phone from the table and led him to what looked like a guest bedroom farthest from the entrance, with the confidence of someone who knew where the guest bedroom would be.

"What's going on?"

This was Luke, trusting me enough to tell him the truth, giving me, what, chance number five to prove I wasn't just inventing things to keep him around, to keep him from seeing me? But the truth was something I'd thrown away long ago. Unlike the milk, it had expired. But my story was starting to congeal. Rain began to pound the roof in waves, its soothing sound threatening me.

Luke knew I had not seen Finn in years (okay, ever) and had never been to his place before (because it did not exist). The story I had told Luke was generously edited. Sometimes redrafted. At one point in it Finn had threatened suicide and I'd made it halfway through the Maine wilderness midwinter, my car hitting old mud ruts, before he'd called me, when I'd finally gotten service and he told me that he was okay. All those details sealing me inside the story as I told it to Luke: the pine needles shedding onto my windshield as I backed into the trunk of a tree, turning around to go home. Those cuts raining down.

I'd told Luke something else, a buffer to the truth, buried so far beneath me: My father's home had been twice ransacked; he'd moved to the middle of Maine for a job finding water for wells and lost the position for no good reason, his four kids each, independently, too busy to visit. But I'd dug dirt over that too—I added to it my father as an alcoholic who routinely reached for tequila at 8 a.m.

Underneath all this? Fine. The honest mistreatment hadn't come from him, but from a teacher in middle school, who in the seventh grade had kissed me against the chalkboard during recess—with the blinds pulled down, I could see through the small line of visibility in one window kids playing on the soccer field as the back of my T-shirt collected chalk from practice problems. When I began to resist, I started getting bad grades. Humiliated in front of the class. Never the right answer. My life nose-dived, a plane engine cut midflight. Whole years wiped away from the crash. My gayness confused my parents, and there was so much blame, in every direction, that it became impossible to explain, pointless to dole out. A knot I couldn't untangle, a knot I was tangled in.

So the story I offered, the glimmering surface of the water, was something I thought Luke would understand, one night over wine, trying to pull him closer to me after imagining him in that theater with someone else. I poured the pain into another cup, with a different story, one in which my father had spit the word "pansy" in my face, holding my wrists down on the twin bed, making a regular show of his homophobic rage, drinking the kind and amount of hard liquor that could "kill a man easy, any day." I told Luke he had died years ago, not just now, and I remembered him tipping out the last residue of the wine from its bottle, right after I had said those words. And how I wanted to start over, but I thought, if there were a way to fall in love, both of us together, whatever real love was, maybe it had the power to erase that story, to make it about us in the now, and not about who I used to be, or who had said what, because I was changing, I really was, and I wasn't sure if he could tell.

And then, this. A free house. "It's gross," my sister insisted. But I indulged Luke, when I told him Finn had finally passed, that moment washing over me in a tropical surf. He told me the visit was part of a healing process, and I wanted more than anything to show him I could heal.

The man's bags hit a door, closer than I expected.

"What the hell is going on?" Luke asked.

"Okay, I don't really know—" I started, but backtracked. I needed to be confident. "Okay, I do know, but this is just going to sound crazy."

"What?" Luke said. He sounded almost defiant. Something in his voice told me he knew I was lying. Or at least heading in that direction.

"Okay. So. Finn, he had some people after him. Old money stuff."

Old money stuff. Seriously? The best I could do.

"Old money stuff?" Luke said. He sat on the bed, which creaked with his weight, so he stood up fast. It made him touchy. I had mentioned bailing Finn out, twice. Where I'd left him, in that story, he was fine, a thick slab of my savings tossed out to him. A life raft I'd in truth needed myself.

"Are they here for something?" Luke asked, confused.

"Probably," I said. "That's probably it."

Luke was getting manic, and it pleased me in a small way that I had the upper hand on reason, or maybe just a moronic sense of calm.

"Do you have everything you came in with?"

Luke paused and looked at me. So dramatic. I wanted to slap him for being such a queen about this. *Grow up*, I thought, and briefly appreciated the irony of that sentiment.

"My camera," Luke said.

The front door creaked open, the screen door snapping shut. The heavy sound of boots on the floor, plastic grocery bags crinkling in the silence.

"Well," Luke whispered loudly, "there's my food."

I doubled down on the concern and gave him a *shhh*.

We moved close to the window, staying low. If worse came to worst—well, I wouldn't know what to do then. The sound of boots stopped, and we froze. A man's voice through chewing—"The fuck is this?"

"My camera. Oh no."

"Why did you even bring that?"

"I thought we could get some pics up here."

"At Finn's place, right after he died. Nice," I said. My allegiance to the lie was so strong this came from a place of reflex, not thought, and for a moment it scared me more than the man, who I guess—lucky us—was staying put in the kitchen. A beer cracked.

"Oh God, what was that?" Luke said, clutching his heart.

"It was literally a beer."

"What in the shit?" the man said to himself. He had found the camera. I listened closely, unsure if, or maybe hoping that, someone else was so deep in their lie, layers and layers down like me, that it was really my father coming home after all these years, unlacing his shoes. It moved me more than I realized to think I might be hiding from exactly him, and it required almost a physical push for me to say no to the idea. No, this man was not my father.

"What was on that camera?" I asked Luke. "Exactly?"

"Us. And some shots from the roof. Can we distract him? What does he want from us?"

"Probably not sex." I laughed, finding it funny.

"Should we bust the window?"

The masculine quality to the words "bust the window"

caught on me for a moment, before it occurred to me this stranger likely had a gun somewhere, maybe on him, maybe like my father did, all those years I didn't call or visit, the glow of the television monitor back on him alone late at night. A chill shot out from my heart. Just as I was about to say, in all seriousness, *Yes, let's break glass and cause a scene*, the boots started toward us.

"If he finds us, we're not a couple," Luke said to me.

The night turned hopeless with a litany of questions, the answers to which I did not have and knew did not exist. What was I trying to save now? Which story did I want the most? The time to choose had long since passed, but it felt still like the time to choose. Maybe there would be another time to choose—days, weeks down the road, back in Boston, a new glass of wine with Luke. The thought pulled me up, a rope down the well of my despair.

A door closed one room over, the sound of a lifted toilet seat.

"Go!" I whispered loudly to Luke, and we crept fast back into the kitchen and got to the door and opened it before Luke swung around and said, full volume, "He has photos of us."

This had not occurred to me at any point either. And then I imagined the fingerprints.

I mean, come on, I asked myself, master inventor of lies, maker of illusion, spell caster of self-sabotage—and you can't get yourself out of this one?

"Call the police," Luke told me. "He's trespassing. On Finn's property. My phone's in the car." We stepped out into the rain, and I watched Luke's hair as it became slick. Everything would have been fine if the man didn't have Luke's camera, which was at the exact moment this thought revealing our identities as intruders in his story.

"I can't. No service," I told Luke. But actually, there was. Three bars of it.

"Let me see your phone," Luke said. "I can maybe get service."

"Do we even need the camera?"

"Let me see your phone!"

"No. He's probably out of the bathroom by now. We need to go—that guy is dangerous."

But the real danger? There was no way out. I had found the last room in our story, the one with no more doors or windows, which I had known was waiting for me this whole time. I told Luke I'd heard—okay, fine, this is a confession? I told Luke about men who used to come to Finn's house, pounding on the door with a pistol. "See these marks?" I said in the useless dark. "We have to go *now*." And they once held him up against the side of this cabin. Splinters in his back. And he looked at me like I was an idiot, because apparently I had told you before that Finn never opened the door for strangers, and how could I even see those marks, and I could feel my father disappearing through all of this telling, and then you saw my phone because you took it from me, and I had to stop you from calling the police, and I told you I was sorry, quietly, and then you asked me what was true. And I think the lightning flashed a branching vein across the sky and the man

turned off a light and everything was suddenly bright before it was suddenly dark and I couldn't see you anymore.
Then I wished I'd entertained my wild idea to cast Finn,
to prove him to be real, to breathe the same air so maybe
with time we could both forget, and not break the glass
like this.

Two gunshots in the night, my heart a trapped animal
inside the trapped animal that was me. And you didn't
even want to hear me confess. You hated the truth, as it
grabbed us by the collar, and so did I. And that's the end.

I didn't get far into all of this before you told me to stop
talking. On the drive home, along the never-ending ocean,
past that circus tent, a dark triangle propped up against the
sky, I said I would write it all down objectively, from my
perspective. So there it is. We are still somewhere up in
Maine together in that camera, though I'm sure you try not
to think about that. And I do have an explanation, though
you said you didn't want one. We tell lies to make ourselves believe the stories we have, to sink them deeper into
us, so we don't forget. So we can't. That's maybe the only
thing I do know.

But here's what I want to know—did you feel it? Taking
those photos with that camera, our backs to the sun, that
salty July air, bare assed on those rocks in Nantucket? A
boat came by with its big white sail waving, and we joked
about swimming out to it and scaring whoever owned it
off and just riding it away? It's like that. Just because we

live inside a lie, doesn't mean we don't feel the truth thrum through us, or that we can't sometimes breathe underwater in it, just for a moment.

I know you can't see it. And I know you know that. But I jumped into the water for you. I swam out and then that boat really was mine, and ever since, I've been trying to find my way back, to find the right port. To stand on solid ground. To finally come, and find you.

PUBLICATION CREDITS

Stories in this collection have appeared in *The Journal*, *Slice*, *The Carolina Quarterly*, *Passages North*, *Devil's Lake*, *Tin House*, *Hobart*, *South Dakota Review*, *Joyland*, and *Ninth Letter*.

ACKNOWLEDGMENTS

Thank you first and foremost to my incredible agent Caroline Eisenmann at Frances Goldin Literary Agency and my extraordinary editor Victoria Savanh at Penguin Books. Your belief in these stories has been unwavering, and I could not be luckier to work with both of you.

To Preston Witt and Brett Beach at *The Journal*, Jennifer Howard and Matt Wienkam at *Passages North*, Lee Ann Roripaugh at *South Dakota Review*, Maisie Cochran and Thomas Ross at *Tin House*, Kyle Lucia Wu and Michelle Lyn King at *Joyland*, Carrie Schuettpelz at *Devil's Lake*, Rae Yan at *The Carolina Quarterly*, Celia Johnson and Maria Gagliano at *Slice Magazine*, Aaron Burch at *Hobart*, Tara Laskowski at *SmokeLong Quarterly*, E. B. Bartels at *Columbia: A Journal of Literature and Art*, Matthew Minicucci at *Ninth Letter*, and Carmen Johnson and Morgan Parker at *Day One*, as well as the dedicated staffs of these journals: Thank you so much for your excellent edits and time with my work.

Thank you also to the brilliant Caedra Scott-Flaherty for providing the morbid inspiration for "Rorschach" with her terrific story "The Channel"—and for her kindness in permitting it to appear in this book. (And for jumpstarting the memory of my time as a nameless apostle in a high school production of *Jesus Christ Superstar*.)

To the following incredible writers, editors, teachers, and friends, whose support and insight has provided boundless opportunity and encouragement, and without whom this book would not have been possible: most notably to Janet Schofield, the best mentor anyone could ask for, whose office I found myself running up to, breathless to discuss some new story, almost daily. Thank you for your patience and guidance. I owe a debt of gratitude to you all: Andy Acosta, Brandon Amico, Armando Arrieta, Sera Bourgeau, Catherine Carberry, Kerry Cullen, Janae Cummings, Billy DiMichele, David Ebershoff, Elizabeth Eslami, Erin Harris, Shayla Lawson, Danielle Lazarin, Halimah Marcus, Alyce Miller, Patrick Nathan, Jodi Picoult, Susan Reynolds, Rosemary Santarelli, Siobhan Senier, Gavin Seyler, Kayla Thomas, Jacinda Townsend, and Jake Zucker.

Thank you to Sara Leonard, Megan Gerrity, Marlene De Jesús, and Gretchen Achilles.

Thank you to the talented, hardworking staff of *Indiana Review*, and copilots Britt Ashley and Su Cho.

To Brick Kyle, whose name even sounds like a lie. For the courage to write this book. For your inspiring brilliance and seeing past every last decoy. This book is for and thanks to you.

Thank you, Mom and Dad. Elisabeth, David, Patrick, Brian. The next one's for all of you, though I pray to God you don't read that either.